# THE WINE OF SOLITUDE

# IRÈNE NÉMIROVSKY

# The Wine
# of Solitude

*Translated from the French by Sandra Smith*

Chatto & Windus
LONDON

Published by Chatto & Windus 2011

2 4 6 8 10 9 7 5 3

First published in France as *Le Vin de solitude* by Éditions Albin Michel in 1935

Copyright © Éditions Albin Michel 1935

Translation copyright © Sandra Smith 2011

The Estate of Irène Némirovsky has asserted her right under the Copyright,
Designs and Patents Act 1988 to be identified as the author of this work

First published in Great Britain in 2011 by
Chatto & Windus
Random House, 20 Vauxhall Bridge Road,
London SW1V 2SA

www.randomhouse.co.uk

Addresses for companies within The Random House Group Limited can be found at:
www.randomhouse.co.uk/offices.htm

The Random House Group Limited Reg. No. 954009

A CIP catalogue record for this book
is available from the British Library

Hardback ISBN 9780701185572
Trade paperback ISBN 9780701185589

The Random House Group Limited supports The Forest Stewardship
Council (FSC®), the leading international forest certification organisation.
Our books carrying the FSC label are printed on FSC® certified paper.
FSC is the only forest certification scheme endorsed by the leading environmental
organisations, including Greenpeace. Our paper procurement policy can be found at
www.randomhouse.co.uk/environment

Typeset by Palimpsest Book Production Limited, Falkirk, Stirlingshire

Printed and bound in Great Britain by Clays Ltd, St Ives plc

# PART I

# 1

In the part of the world where Hélène Karol was born, dusk began with a thick cloud of dust that swirled slowly in the air before drifting to the ground, bringing the damp night with it. A hazy, reddish light lingered low in the sky; the wind brought the smell of the Ukrainian plains to the city, a mild yet bitter scent of smoke, cold water and rushes that grew along the riverbanks. The wind blew in from Asia; it had pushed its way between the Ural Mountains and the Caspian Sea; it brought with it whirls of yellow dust that cracked between the teeth; it was dry and biting; it filled the air with a howl that faded as it disappeared towards the west. Then all was calm. The setting sun, pale and dull, veiled behind whitish clouds, sank deep into the river.

From the Karols' balcony you could see the whole town, from the Dnieper River to the hills in the distance; its outline was marked out by the gaslights that lined the winding streets with their fluttering little flames, while on the opposite bank the first fires of spring smouldered in the grass.

The balcony was surrounded by boxes full of flowers that had been especially chosen because they opened at night, Nicotiana, Sweet Mignonette, Tuberoses; the balcony was so wide that it could hold the dining table and chairs, a wicker 'love-seat' and the armchair of Safronov, Hélène's grandfather.

The family sat around the table, eating in silence; the flame from the gas lamp attracted delicate moths with beige wings. Leaning forward, Hélène could see the acacias in the courtyard, lit up in the moonlight. The courtyard was bare and dirty but lined with trees and flowers, like a garden. On summer evenings the servants sat down there, talking and laughing among themselves; sometimes a white skirt could be seen moving about in the darkness; they could hear an accordion playing and a muffled cry: 'Let go of me, you devil!'

'Well, they're not bored down there . . .' said Madame Karol, looking up.

Hélène was half asleep in her chair. At this time of year, they ate late; she could feel her legs trembling, aching from having run around the garden; her chest rose and fell quickly as she remembered the shrill cries she couldn't help but make as she ran after the hoop, cries like the song of some bird. Her small rough hand loved touching her favourite black ball, which she had hidden in the pocket of her light cotton dress even though it left bruises as it pressed into her leg. She was eight years old; she wore a dress of broderie anglaise with a white silk belt tied below her waist in a 'butterfly' bow fixed in place with two pins. Bats flew by and as each one swooped down low, Mademoiselle Rose, Hélène's French governess, let out a little cry and laughed.

Hélène half opened her tired eyes and looked at her family.

Her father's face was surrounded by a sort of yellowish haze that shimmered like a halo: to her weary eyes it looked as if the light from the lamp was flickering, but yes, it really *was* flickering. The lamp had begun to smoke; Hélène's grandmother shouted to the servant, 'Macha! Lower the lamp!'

Hélène's mother sighed, yawned and flicked through Paris fashion magazines while she ate.

Hélène's father said nothing, softly drumming his slim, delicate fingers on the table.

He was the only one whom Hélène resembled; she looked exactly like him. It was from him she had inherited her passionate eyes, wide mouth, curly hair and swarthy complexion that turned almost yellow whenever she was sad or ill. She looked at him tenderly. But he only had eyes for his wife. His loving caresses were only for her too.

She pushed away his hand. 'Don't, Boris,' she said, sullen and irritable. 'It's hot, leave me be . . .'

She pulled the lamp towards her, leaving the others in darkness; she sighed with boredom and weariness, curling strands of her hair round her fingers. She was a tall, shapely woman 'of regal bearing' and with a tendency to plumpness, which she fought by using corsets shaped liked breastplates, as was the fashion; her breasts nestled in two satin pockets, like fruit in a basket. Her arms were white and powdered. Hélène felt a strange sensation, close to revulsion, when she saw her mother's snow-white skin, pale, languid hands and claw-like nails. Hélène's grandfather completed the family circle.

The moon spilled its tranquil light over the tops of the lime trees; nightingales sang beyond the hills. The Dnieper shimmered a dazzling white. The moonlight shone on the nape of Madame Karol's neck, which was as pale and hard as marble;

it reflected off Boris Karol's silvery hair and the short, tapered beard of the elderly Safronov; it cast a dim light on the small, wrinkled, angular features of her grandmother: she was only fifty but she looked so old, so weary . . . The silence of this sleepy provincial town, lost deep within Russia, was intense, heavy and overwhelmingly sad. Then, suddenly, the stillness was broken by the sound of a carriage jolting along the paved street: the terrible din of a lashing whip, swearing, the bump of wheels against stone, which faded and disappeared into the distance . . . Nothing more . . . silence . . . just the rustling of birds' wings in the trees . . . the sound of a distant song from some country road, interrupted by the noise of arguments, shouting, the thud of a policeman's boots, the screams of a drunken woman being dragged to the police station by the hair . . . Silence once more . . .

Hélène gently pinched her arms so she wouldn't fall asleep; her cheeks burned as if they were on fire. Her dark curls kept her neck warm; she ran her fingers through her hair, lifting it up; she thought angrily that it was only her long hair that kept her from beating the boys when they raced: they grabbed it while she was running; she smiled with pride recalling how she had kept her balance on the slippery edge of the fountain. Her arms and legs were racked with agonising but exhilarating exhaustion; she secretly rubbed her painful knees, covered in scratches and bruises; her passionate blood pulsed quietly, deep within her body; she kicked the underside of the table impatiently, hammering its wood and sometimes her grandmother's legs, who said nothing so Hélène wouldn't be scolded.

'Put your hands on the table,' Madame Karol said sharply. Then she continued reading her fashion magazine.

'Tea-gown in lemon-yellow twilled silk with eighteen orange velvet bows to fasten the bodice . . .' she said with a sigh, forming each word with longing.

She wound a curl of her shiny dark hair round her fingers and stroked it against her cheek as if in a dream. She was bored: she didn't like meeting up with other women to smoke and play cards, as they all did as soon as they were over thirty. Looking after the house and her child filled her with horror. She was only happy in a hotel, in a room with a bed and a trunk, in Paris . . .

'Ah, Paris!' she thought, closing her eyes. 'To eat at the bar of the Chauffeurs' Café, to sleep in a train compartment, even if necessary on the hard benches in third class, but to be alone and free!' Here, from every window, the women looked her up and down, glaring at her Parisian dresses, her make-up, the man she was with. Here, every married woman had a lover, whom the children called 'Uncle' and who played cards with their husbands. 'Why bother having a lover at all, then?' she thought, remembering the men who followed her around in Paris, men she didn't know . . . That, at least, was exciting, dangerous, thrilling . . . To hold a man tightly in her arms when she didn't even know his name or where he came from, a man she would never see again, that and that alone gave her the sharp thrill of pleasure she desired.

'Ah,' she thought, 'I wasn't destined to be a placid middle-class woman, satisfied with her husband and child.'

They had finished their meal; Karol pushed away his plate and set out the roulette wheel purchased the previous year in Nice. Everyone gathered round him: he threw the ivory ball almost angrily, but every now and again, when the sound of the accordion echoed more loudly from the courtyard, he would raise his long finger in the air and, without interrupting his game of roulette, he would hum the tune they played with extreme accuracy, then softly whistle it through his half-open lips.

'Do you remember Nice, Hélène?' said Madame Karol.

Hélène did remember Nice.

'And Paris? You haven't forgotten Paris, have you?'

Hélène felt her heart melt with tenderness at the memory of Paris, the Tuileries Gardens . . . (Trees the colour of tarnished steel beneath the tender winter sky, the sweet smell of the rain, and in the heavy, misty dusk, the yellowish moon that rose slowly above the column in the Place Vendôme . . .)

Karol had forgotten everyone else around him. He drummed his fingers nervously on the table and watched the little ivory ball wildly spin and sway. 'Black, red, the 2, the 8 . . . Ah! I would have won . . . Forty-four times what I'd bet. And with just one gold louis.'

But it was over almost too quickly. There wasn't time to enjoy the uncertainty or the danger, the despair in defeat or the exhilaration of victory. Baccarat, now there was an idea . . . But he was still too poor for that, too unimportant. One day, perhaps . . .

'Ah, dear God,' the elderly Madame Safronov murmured. 'Ah, dear God!' It was an habitual refrain. She had a slight limp in one leg, but walked quickly: her features were faded, washed out by her tears, like a very old photograph; her yellowish wrinkled neck sat above the frilled little collar of her white blouse. She continually brought her hand to rest against her flat chest, as if every word she said would make her heart pound; she was always sad, complaining, anxious:

everything was an excuse for her to sigh, to lament. 'Life is bad,' she would say. 'God is terrible. Men are harsh . . .'

She turned to her daughter. 'You're right, you know, Bella. Enjoy life while you're still in good health. Eat something. Do you want some of this? A bit of that? Do you want my chair, my knife, my bread, my food? Take it . . . Take it, Boris, and you, Bella, and you, George, and you my darling Hélène . . .' Take my time, my care, my blood, my flesh . . . she seemed to be saying as she stared at them with her soft, dead eyes.

But everyone pushed her away. Then she would shake her head affectionately and force herself to smile. 'All right, all right, I'll be quiet, I won't say anything . . .'

Meanwhile, George Safronov had sat up straighter, lifting his tall, dry body and bald head, while carefully examining his fingernails. He polished them twice a day: all morning long, and once before the evening meal. He was not interested in the conversation of women. Boris Karol was a peasant. 'He should consider himself very lucky to have married Safronov's daughter . . .' He opened out his newspaper.

Hélène read the word 'War'. 'Is there going to be a war, Grandfather?' she asked.

'What?'

Whenever she opened her mouth, everyone eyed her scornfully and waited a moment before speaking, firstly to find out her mother's opinion on what she'd said and then presumably because she was so unimportant, so young, that they felt they had to travel a great distance just to reach her.

'War? And where have you heard talk of . . . ? Oh! Maybe, no one knows . . .'

'I really hope not,' said Hélène, sensing it was what she was supposed to say.

They all looked at her and laughed nervously; her father smiled with a tender, melancholy, mocking expression.

'What a clever thing to say,' said Bella dismissively. 'If there's a war, fabric will be more expensive . . . You do know that Papa owns a textile factory, don't you?'

She laughed but without opening her mouth: her thin lips formed a harsh line that cut across her face and were always pinched, either to make her mouth seem smaller, or to hide the gold tooth at the back, or because she wanted to look refined. She raised her head and noticed the clock: 'Time for bed. Off you go . . .'

Her grandmother put out her arm when Hélène walked past; her anxious eyes and weary face grew tense. 'Give Grandma a hug and a kiss . . .' And when the impatient, ungrateful, deeply irritated child allowed herself to be held for a moment by the thin old woman, she crushed Hélène to her breast with all her might.

The only kiss Hélène accepted and returned with joy was her father's. She felt related and close to him alone, part of his flesh and blood, sharing his soul, his strength, his weaknesses. He leaned down towards her with his silvery white hair that looked almost green in the moonlight; his face was still young, but wrinkled, furrowed by cares; his eyes were sometimes intense and sad, sometimes lit up with the fire of mischievous cheerfulness; he tugged playfully at her hair. 'Goodnight, Lenoussia, my little one . . .'

She left them, and at that very instant serenity and joy, along with pure and simple affection, returned to her heart; she held Mademoiselle Rose's hand in hers. She went to bed and fell asleep. Mademoiselle Rose sat sewing in the golden beam of the lamp; its light shone across her thin, bare little hand. A shaft of moonlight pushed through the white ruched blind. Mademoiselle Rose was lost in thought. 'Hélène needs new dresses, pinafores, socks . . . Hélène is growing up too quickly . . .'

Occasionally a noise, a flash of lightning, the shadow of a bat, a cockroach on the white stove made her shudder. 'I'll never get used to this place,' she sighed. 'Never . . .'

# 2

Hélène was sitting on the floor in her bedroom, playing. It was a warm, clear spring evening; the pale sky was like a crystal ball with the glowing traces of a pink fire at its heart. Through the half-open door of the sitting room, the child could hear the sound of a French ballad. Bella was singing; when she wasn't polishing her nails, when she wasn't sighing from sadness and boredom, stretched out in the dining room on the old settee whose stuffing was sticking through the fabric in little tufts, she would sit at the piano and sing, accompanying herself with the odd lethargic chord. When she came to the words 'love' or 'lover', her voice sounded more passionate and clear; she was no longer afraid to open her mouth wide; she didn't pinch her lips together; she sang out those words of love and her voice took on a sweet, husky tone that was unlike its normally bitter or weary sound. Hélène, who had quietly stepped into the room, watched her in surprised silence.

The sitting-room walls were covered in a cotton fabric that was meant to look like silk; it had once been flesh-coloured but was now dusty and drab. This rough cotton material was manufactured at the factory where Karol was the manager; it smelled of glue and fruit, and the local women used it to make their Sunday dresses and headscarves. But the furniture came from Paris, from the Faubourg Saint-Antoine: ottomans covered in green and raspberry velvet, torchères in carved wood, Japanese lanterns fringed with coloured beads. A lamp lit up the nail buffer absent-mindedly left on top of the piano. Bella's nails sparkled under the light; they were round and curved with sharp tips, like claws. In the rare moments when she displayed any maternal affection, pressing her daughter to her breast, her nails almost always scratched Hélène's bare arm or face.

The child inched her way into the room. Sometimes Bella stopped playing and fell silent; with her hands resting on the keyboard, she seemed to be waiting, listening, her heart full of hope. But from outside came nothing but the indifferent silence of the spring evening and the sound of the impatient wind pushing along the endless yellow dust from Asia.

'When – it's – all – over,' sighed Madame Karol. Hélène watched the way she clamped her teeth together; it was as if she were eating a piece of fruit; her wide, bright eyes that seemed so harsh, so empty, beneath the curve of her slim eyebrows, were full of tears: sparkling water that welled up but never spilled over.

Hélène went and stood against the window, looking out into the street. Occasionally she would see an old carriage pulled by two slow-moving horses, driven by a coachman dressed in the Polish fashion: velvet waistcoat, puffy red sleeves and peacock feathers in his hat; it was Bella's aunt, a Safronov from the older generation, a branch of the family that had kept its wealth, that hadn't squandered its fortune, that didn't need to marry off its daughters to insignificant little Jews who managed factories in the poor part of town. Lydia Safronov was thin and stiff with dried-out yellowish skin and shining dark eyes; her chest was ravaged by cancer, which she suffered with a sort of aggressive resignation; always cold, she wrapped herself in an ample, regal fur coat. On seeing her niece, Lydia Safronov would barely deign to nod in icy acknowledgement, her mouth pinched close and her face wearing an expression that was impenetrable, distant and full of bitter, cruel scorn. Sometimes her son Max sat next to her; he was still a thin young boy dressed in the grey uniform worn in secondary school; his cap bore the symbol of the Imperial eagle; he held his little head very high atop his long, fragile neck, with the same harsh and haughty attitude as his mother; he had a delicate hooked nose and seemed aware of its fine quality, just as he was aware of the lush richness of the horses, the carriage, and the quality of the expensive English rug covering his knees; his eyes were cold with a faraway look in them. Whenever they ran into each other in the street, Mademoiselle Rose would give Hélène a little nudge, and she would curtsey, lowering her head in a sullen manner; her cousin would briefly acknowledge her before turning away, and her aunt looked at her with pity through a gold lorgnette that sparkled in the sunlight.

But on this day, only one carriage passed slowly beneath the window; a woman was inside; she was holding a child's coffin tightly to her breast, as if it were a bundle of clothing; this was how the poor people avoided paying for funerals. The woman's face looked peaceful; she was chewing some sunflower seeds; she was smiling, doubtless happy to have one less mouth to feed, one less cry to break the silence of the night.

Suddenly the door opened and Hélène's father came into the room.

Bella shuddered, quickly closing the piano, and looked anxiously at her husband. He never came home this early from the factory. For the first time in her life, Hélène saw her father's face twitch slightly, a twitch that pulled his hollow cheeks to the side and which would come to represent for her the first sign of disaster, the mark of defeat on a man's face, for Boris Karol never knew any other way to show he was upset, not then and not later, when he became old and ill.

He walked into the middle of the room, seemed to hesitate, then said with a little harsh, forced laugh, 'Bella, I've lost my job.'

'What?' she cried.

He shrugged his shoulders and answered curtly, 'You heard me.'

'You've been let go?'

Karol pursed his lips. 'That's right,' he said after a pause.

'But why? Why? What did you do?'

'Nothing,' he said in a hoarse, weary voice, and Hélène felt a strange sense of pity as she heard the irritated little sigh that escaped through his clenched teeth. He lowered himself into a chair, the one nearest to him, and sat there motionless, his back hunched and arms dangling, looking down at the ground and whistling without realising it.

'Nothing!' Bella shouted, making him jump. 'You must be mad! What did he say? What happened? But we'll be penniless!'

She twisted her arms together with a sudden, supple movement that reminded Hélène of the serpents on the Medusa's head she was drawing for her art teacher. From the delicate, convulsed mouth words, sighs and curses came flooding out: 'What did you do, Boris? You have no right to hide anything from me! You have a family, a child! You weren't let go for no reason! Did you play the stock market? I knew it! Admit it, go on, admit it! No? Well, then, did you lose money playing cards? At least say something, admit what happened, say something! Ah, you're killing me!'

Hélène had slipped out through the open door. She went back to her room and sat down on the floor. She had heard them fighting so many times in her short life that she wasn't overly concerned. They would shout, then they would stop. Nevertheless, her heart was heavy and tight in her chest.

'The director called me in to see him,' she heard him continue, 'and since you want to know, Bella, he wanted to talk to me about you. Wait a moment. He told me you spent too much money. Just wait. You can have your say afterwards. He talked about your dresses, your trips abroad, which, according to him, I couldn't possibly pay for on my salary. He told me that the money I had easy access to was a temptation he didn't want to inflict on me. I asked him if a single penny had disappeared. "No," he said, but it was inevitable that one day it would, if your lifestyle didn't change. I warned you, Bella, remember? Every time you bought a new dress or fur coat, every time you left for Paris, I said it over and over again: "Be careful, we live in a small town. People talk. I'll be accused of stealing." The director of the factory lives in Moscow. It's natural that he must be able to trust me, and he can't trust me. I would have done the same if I were in his shoes. I can't refuse you anything. I can't bear it when a woman nags and cries. I'd rather give in; I'd rather people take me for a coward, a thief, a hen-pecked husband, because, in the end, another man might suspect that . . . Be quiet,' he shouted suddenly, and his rough, wild voice drowned out what Bella was saying. 'Be quiet! I know exactly what you're going to tell me. Yes, I trust you. Don't say a word! I don't want to know. You are my wife. My wife, my child, my house . . . When all is said and done, you're all I have. Of course I have to take care of you,' he said softly.

'But Boris, what are you saying? Do you realise what you're implying? Boris, my darling . . .'

'Be quiet . . .'

'I have nothing to hide . . .'

'Be quiet!'

'Ah! You don't love me any more; you would never have spoken to me like this a few years ago. Remember? I was a Safronov; I could have married anyone I liked. Then you came along. Remember the scandal our marriage caused? All those people saying to me, "*You! You* marrying that little Jew who came out of nowhere, who wandered around Lord knows where, whose family you don't even know! *You*!?" But I loved you, Boris.'

'You didn't have a penny and all your other boyfriends wanted a dowry,' he said bitterly. 'And I'm the one who feeds your mother and father, and puts a roof over their heads, me, the little Jew who came out of nowhere: *I'm* the one who pays for all the Safronovs, *me, me* . . . To hell with all of you!'

'But I loved you, Boris, I loved you! I still love you! I'm faithful to you, I . . .'

'Enough!' he said in despair. 'I don't want to talk about that. It's got nothing to do with it. You're my wife and I have to believe in my wife. Otherwise there would be nothing left that was decent, nothing, nothing at all. Not another word about it, Bella, not another word!'

'It's those jealous women, those envious old women all around us who can't forgive me because I'm happy, because they know that I'm happy! They can't forgive me for having a husband like you, for being young and attractive! They're the ones who've caused all this trouble!'

'Perhaps,' Karol said weakly.

She could tell he was weakening by the tone of his voice and immediately dissolved into floods of tears.

'I would never have believed you could speak so harshly to me, say such hurtful things to me . . . I'll never forgive you, never! I do everything possible to make you happy . . . You're the only one I have in the world, after all, and I'm the only one you have!'

'What's the point in talking about that?' Karol said once more, his voice weary and tinged with pain and embarrassment. 'You know that I love you.'

In spite of the closed door, Hélène could hear every word. But she pretended not to be listening: she was building a fortress for her toy soldiers out of a stack of old books. Her grandmother crossed the room without making a sound; she was sighing and tears ran down her elderly face, but Hélène thought nothing of it: her grandmother was always crying; her eyes were constantly red, her lips trembling. Mademoiselle Rose was sewing in silence; Hélène gave her a mischievous look.

'They're shouting . . . Can you hear? What's going on?'

Mademoiselle Rose said nothing at first; she pursed her lips and pushed her needle hard through the hem that sat across her knee. 'You shouldn't listen, Lili,' she said finally.

'I'm not listening. I just can't help hearing them.'

'Those hideous women,' Bella shouted through her tears, 'those old, fat, ugly creatures who can't forgive me for having hats and dresses from Paris. *They* all have lovers, you know they do, Boris. And to think of all the men who chase after me and whom I turn away . . .'

'Get up from the floor,' said Mademoiselle Rose.

When her parents fell silent, for their quarrel was constantly interrupted by sudden moments of calm when they paused to gather their strength in order better to rip each other apart, Hélène could hear the servants singing as they ironed at the back of the kitchen, and it occurred to her that she could sense with more acuity than usual the strange, luminous silence of the evening. But what most interested her at that moment was her fortress. Despite the fact that the wooden soldiers had been chewed by the dogs, and their red tunics stained Hélène's dress and fingers, she loved to arrange them; to her, they were the Grenadiers of the Imperial Army, Napoleon's Guards. Bent over, her curls brushing the ground, she breathed in the musty odour of the dusty old wooden floor. Several large books, their pages open, had been set up to create a dark, threatening gorge between the mountains where the army was hiding out among fallen rocks. She placed two sentries at the entrance. She quickly piled the remaining books one on top of the other and started reciting sentences to herself from the *Mémorial de Sainte-Hélène*, her favourite book; she knew it almost by heart.

Mademoiselle Rose had gone to sit by the window to sew

in the fading daylight. How sleepy and calm the world seemed with the peaceful cooing of the ringdoves on the rooftop, while from the room next door she could hear her mother's tears, sobs, sighs and curses . . .

Hélène stood up and put her hand into the opening of her dress: 'Field Marshals, officers, soldiers . . .' She was standing in the Wagram battlefield, surrounded by the dead. She pictured the scene so clearly that she could have drawn the field covered in yellowing grass cropped by the horses. A dream of bloodshed, of glory held her motionless, transfixed, a little girl with her mouth wide open, her lower lip drooping, her dishevelled hair falling over her damp forehead; her painful tonsils made it difficult to breathe, but nevertheless, each of her hoarse breaths echoed her deepest thoughts. She revelled in imagining the small green hilltop in the setting sun where she was both the Emperor (soundlessly her lips formed the words, 'Soldiers, you have earned everlasting glory!') and at the same time the young lieutenant who lay dying while pressing his lips to the golden fringes of the French flag. Blood trickled from his pierced breast. In the mirror of the wardrobe she could see a little eight-year-old girl in a blue dress and a large white smock; her pale face wore a dazed expression that reflected the turbulence of her inner life; her fingers were stained with ink, and she had strong, solid legs in thick tights and heavy lace-up boots. But Hélène didn't recognise her. In order better to hide her secret dream, better to throw anyone who might discover it off the scent, she began singing quietly through half-open lips: '*There was a little ship . . .*'

Outside, a woman leaned over the low wall of the court-yard and shouted, 'Hey! Aren't you ashamed to be chasing after women at your age, you old scoundrel?'

In the distance, the bells from the monastery rang loudly, solemnly, through the clear evening air.

'. . . *That had ne-ne-never sailed* . . .'

The soldiers attacked; the sky was crimson; the drums were beating.

'When you get back home, your children will say, "He was a soldier in Napoleon's Army."'

'What's going to happen to us, Boris? What's going to happen to us?'

'Why are you feeling sorry for yourself?' her father asked, his voice soft and weary. 'Have you ever wanted for anything? Do you think I'm worried about earning a living? I'm not a layabout like your father. Ever since I was old enough to work, I've never asked anything of anyone . . .'

'No woman is more unhappy than me!'

This time, mysteriously, the words seeped into Hélène's consciousness, filling her heart with bitter resentment. 'Why does she always have to make such a scene,' she thought.

'Unhappy, really?' shouted Karol. 'And what about me? Do you think I'm happy? Why didn't I just bash my skull in on our wedding day, instead of marrying you? I wanted to have a peaceful home, a child. And all I have is you and your shouting and not even a son.'

'Oh, stop it,' thought Hélène. This fight was going on too long, and it seemed more serious and bitter than usual. She kicked the soldiers away and they rolled underneath the furniture.

But she could still hear her mother's fearful, cajoling voice. Usually when Karol shouted at her she would remain quiet, or simply weep and moan.

'Come on now, don't be angry. I'm not blaming you for

anything. Here we are fighting with each other . . . Let's try to think instead. What are you going to do?'

They were speaking more quietly; she couldn't hear any more.

The woman leaning over the wall ran off, laughing: 'You're too old, my dear, too old . . .'

Hélène went over to Mademoiselle Rose and absent-mindedly tugged at her sewing.

Mademoiselle Rose sighed and fixed the bow that was falling over Hélène's forehead: 'You're so hot, Lili. Have a rest now, don't start reading, you read too much; play with your puzzle or your pick-up-sticks . . .'

The servant brought in a lamp and, with the doors and windows shut, a sweet, safe little universe once more encircled the child and her governess, a world that was like a seashell, and just as fragile.

# 3

Mademoiselle Rose was thin and delicate, with a sweet face and fine features; she must have been rather beautiful when she was young, graceful and cheerful, but now she looked thin and worn out; her small mouth was full of the kind of wrinkles caused by bitterness and suffering that mark the lips of women over thirty; she had the beautiful, lively dark eyes of Frenchwomen from the Midi, chestnut hair that was frizzy and as light as smoke and that she wore, in the fashion of the time, in a high crown on top of her smooth forehead; her skin was soft and she smelled of fine soap and violets. She wore a narrow velvet ribbon round her neck, short-sleeved tops of white linen or fine black wool, straight skirts and button-up boots with long, pointy tips. She was rather vain when it came to her small feet and her shapely waist that she pulled tightly in with a suede belt decorated with a dull silver buckle. She was calm and wise, very sensible and modest; for many years she had retained an innocent cheerfulness, despite the apprehension and sadness she felt about Hélène's strange, wild nature, about this chaotic household in this untamed country. Hélène loved only her, no one else. In the evening, when the lamp was lit, Hélène would sit at her little desk and draw or cut out pictures, while Mademoiselle Rose talked about her childhood, her brothers and sisters, the games they had played and the Ursuline convent where she had been raised.

'When I was little I was called Rosette . . .'

'Were you good?'

'Not always.'

'Better than me?'

'You're very good, Hélène, except now and again. You'd think you sometimes had a demon in you.'

'Am I intelligent?'

'Yes, but you think you're more intelligent than you are . . . which won't make you any better or any happier. You must be good and brave. Not to do extraordinary things, you're just an ordinary little girl. But to accept God's will.'

'Yes. But Mama's evil, isn't she?'

'What an idea, Hélène . . . She's not evil; it's just that she has always been spoiled – by her mother, then by your father, who loves her so much, and also spoiled by life. She has never had to work or give in to anyone . . . Come, now, try to draw my picture . . .'

'I can't. Sing, won't you, Mademoiselle Rose, please.'

'You know all my songs.'

'That doesn't matter. Sing "You may have taken Alsace and Lorraine but in spite of you we will always be French".'

Mademoiselle Rose sang often; her voice wasn't very strong but it was clear and melodious. She would sing 'Marlbrough is off to war', 'Love's pleasures last but a moment' and 'I sigh beneath your window, day will soon be here' . . . When she said the word 'love', she, too, sometimes sighed and stroked Hélène's hair. Had she ever been in love? Had she lost the man she'd loved? Had she been happy once? Why had she come to Russia to look after other people's children? Hélène was never to know the answer to these questions. As a little girl she didn't dare ask and, later on, she wished to keep intact within her heart the memory of the only pure, peaceful woman she had ever known, a woman free from the stain of desire, whose eyes seemed only to have looked upon smiling, innocent faces.

Once, Mademoiselle Rose, lost in a daydream, had murmured, 'When I was twenty I was so unhappy that one day I almost threw myself into the Seine.' Her eyes had gone dark and impenetrable, and Hélène sensed that Mademoiselle Rose was so lost in memory that it had become possible to talk of such sad things from the past even to a child, especially to a child. A strange, primitive sense of embarrassment filled the young girl's heart. She could make out all the words she hated on Mademoiselle Rose's trembling lips: 'love', 'kisses', 'fiancé' . . .

Abruptly she had pushed her chair away and begun singing at the top of her voice, swaying backwards and forwards while stamping her feet against the floor. Mademoiselle Rose had looked at her with surprise and melancholy resignation; she had sighed and fallen silent.

'Do sing, Mademoiselle Rose, please. Sing the "Marseillaise". You know, the couplet about the little children: "We shall enter into the fray / when our elders have passed away . . ." Oh, how I long to be French!'

'You're right, Lili. It's the most beautiful country in the world . . .'

Hélène had often gone to bed during her parents' quarrels, to the sound of china being broken, but thanks to Mademoiselle Rose, she could detach herself from the noise of the faraway storm, knowing that she had a peaceful refuge beside this calm young woman who sewed in the lamplight. It was like hearing the sound of the wind in a warm house whose windows are closed.

She could hear Bella's voice: 'If it weren't for the child, I'd leave you! I'd leave right now!'

She would often say this when her husband got annoyed. Occasionally Karol got irritated if he found the house in a mess, or when she had bought a new hat with a pink feather, and it was sitting in its box on the table while the roast was burning or the tablecloth needed mending. But Bella said she had never claimed to be a good housekeeper; she hated everything to do with housework and only lived to enjoy herself. 'That's how I am. You'll just have to take me as I am,' she would say.

Boris Karol would shout, and then stop shouting, for quarrelling made the burden of this marriage, balanced painfully on his shoulders, fall off and roll on to the ground, and it was easier to avoid this: to resign himself to bearing it, rather than having to bend down and heave it back up on to his shoulders once more. He also vaguely feared her threat: 'I'll leave you.' He knew men chased after her, that men found her attractive. He loved her . . .

'Good Lord,' thought Hélène, half asleep, her long legs pushing against the end of the small wooden bed that got no bigger even though she did, and which every year they forgot to replace. She snuggled up under a satin quilt with delicate stitching which, despite the fact that Mademoiselle

Rose mended it almost every day, was losing its stuffing. 'Good Lord, I wish she would just hurry up and leave so they stop talking about it! If only she would die!'

Every night when she said her prayers ('Dear God, please keep Papa and Mama safe and sound . . .'), she replaced, in murderous hope, her mother's name with that of Mademoiselle Rose.

'What's the point of shouting and making useless threats?' she thought. 'Why talk just for the sake of it? That woman is impossible; she's the cross I have to bear.'

When she was talking to herself, Hélène used words that grown-ups used, words that were mature and wise, and came naturally to her, but she would have been too embarrassed to say them aloud, just as she would have found it ridiculous to walk around in grown-up finery; when she spoke, she had to translate her words into simpler, less elegant sentences, which made her sound rather hesitant and gave her a slight stutter that irritated her mother.

'Sometimes this child seems like an idiot. You'd think she had landed on earth from the moon!'

When she was asleep, though, sleep, merciful sleep brought her back to her true age: her dreams were full of movement, energy and cries of joy.

Some while later, Karol went away and the evenings became peaceful once more. He had found a job managing a group of gold mines deep in the Siberian forest. It was the beginning of a road that would lead him to wealth. Meanwhile the house was empty. Only Grandmother stayed at home, silently wandering from one room to another, while her husband and daughter each went their own way as soon as dinner was over. Hélène enjoyed the kind of sweet, exhilarating sleep of childhood that immerses you in a pool of invigorating peace. When she woke up, the room was filled with sunshine. Mademoiselle Rose was dusting the chipped old furniture. She wore a pleated black sateen apron that protected her clothing, but underneath she was already neatly dressed in the corset and short boots she wore to town, the collar of her blouse held closed by a little gold brooch and her hair done. Never was her hair dishevelled, nor did she ever wear a loose-fitting dressing gown or those shape-less skirts that hung from the fat Russian women. She was tidy, precise, meticulous, a little 'aloof', somewhat scornful: a Frenchwoman through and through. She never fussed; she rarely kissed anyone. 'Do I love you? Of course, I love you, when you're a good girl.' But her life revolved around Hélène; the curling of her hair, the dresses she made for her, the meals, games and walks she supervised. She never moral-ised; she gave only the simplest, most ordinary advice: 'Hélène, don't read while you're putting on your socks. One thing at a time.'

'Hélène, tidy up your things: you must learn how to be an organised woman, my darling. Keep your things in order and later on you will have order in your life, and the people who have to live with you will love you for it.'

And so the mornings passed; but little by little, as lunch-time approached, Hélène's heart began to grow heavier and heavier.

Mademoiselle Rose would brush Hélène's curls while saying quietly, 'Make sure you behave during the meal. Your mother is in a bad mood.'

Karol had been gone for such a long time that Hélène was beginning to forget what he looked like; she didn't even know where he was exactly. She had been left in her mother's hands.

How Hélène hated these lunches. How many meals had ended in tears . . . Much later, when she recalled the dingy, dusty dining room, she would also remember the salty taste of the tears that welled up in her eyes and spilled down her face to fall in drops on to her plate, blending with the taste of the food. For a long time, meat had a slight taste of salt to her and bread was moist with bitterness.

The balcony blocked out the sad winter's day; its light barely filtered through into the dining room. She would stare at the old imitation tapestries nailed to the walls, her eyes clouded over with tears that she held back out of pride, tears that made her voice quiver with sadness. When she was older she could never manage to recall her childhood days without also feeling those old tears filling her heart once more.

'Sit up straight . . . Close your mouth . . . Just look at you . . . You look as if you've just been slapped with your mouth open and your bottom lip drooping . . . I do believe this child is turning into an idiot! . . . Pay attention; you're going to knock over your glass! See, what did I tell you? . . . Now you've broken it . . . Here come the tears again . . . Yes, of course, *you* always make excuses for her! . . . Very well then, that's just fine; I'll no longer concern myself with Mademoiselle Hélène's education, let Mademoiselle Hélène have the table manners of a peasant if that's what she wants; I won't get involved any more . . . Look at your mother when she's talking to you . . . Look at me, will you? . . . And it's for this, for *this* that I make sacrifices, for this that I gave up my youth, the best time of my life! . . .' said Madame Karol, thinking with bitterness of this little girl she was forced to drag with her all over Europe, because otherwise you could be sure that she would barely reach Berlin before she would get an hysterical telegram from Grandmother – 'Come back. The child is ill.' – a cold or a sore throat forcing her to retrace the steps she'd only made the night before, and with so much pleasure. The child . . . The child . . . It was all they ever talked about, all of them: her husband, her parents, her friends: 'You have to make sacrifices for your child . . . Think of your child, Bella . . .'

A child, a living reproach, an embarrassment . . . She was well cared for. What else did she need? Later on, wouldn't even she be better off having a young mother who understood life? 'My own mother spent her whole life complaining. Was that any better?' she thought, remembering with bitterness the gloomy house, a woman who was old before her time, her eyes red from crying, who said nothing but 'Eat. Don't wear yourself out. Don't run . . .' A drooling old woman who stifled all joy and love, who prevented the young from enjoying life . . . 'I wasn't happy,' she mused, 'so they can at least let me be happy now; I'm not hurting anyone. When I'm old I'll be calm and wise,' she said, for old age was still so far away . . .

They had finished lunch. But for Hélène the hardest part was still to come: she had to kiss the pale face she so hated, and which always felt cold to her burning lips; she had to place her closed mouth against the cheek she wanted to lacerate with her nails, then perhaps say, 'I'm sorry, Mama.'

She could feel a strange sense of self-pride shudder and bleed within her, as if a more mature soul was trapped within her child's body, and this offended soul was suffering.

'You won't even say sorry, will you? Oh! Please, for heaven's sake, don't bother. I don't want an apology that comes from your lips but not from your heart. Go away.'

But sometimes the scene finished with an inexplicable surge of maternal affection in Bella. 'This child . . . After all, she's all I have . . . Men are so egotistical . . . Later on she'll be my friend, my little companion . . .'

'Come on now, Hélène, don't make such a face. You shouldn't be so resentful. I scolded you, you cried, it's all over now, forgotten. Come and kiss your mother.'

Normally she wasn't at home for the evening meal. Before going to bed, Grandfather Safronov would walk slowly round the sombre sitting room, lit up only by the cold winter moon; he dragged his leg along as he walked, leaning on Hélène's shoulder; he would stroke the fresh rose he wore in his buttonhole, both winter and summer. The piano with its closed lid shone in a pool of light, and the same ray of light made the handsome old man's bald head shine like an egg. He taught Hélène poetry by Victor Hugo, recited pages from Chateaubriand to her. Certain phrases, his solemn, melancholy rhythm, were to remain inexorably linked in her mind to the memory of his heavy, irregular walk, the weight of his bony hand, still delicate and beautiful, as it sat on her shoulder.

Then, once again, to end the long day – a child's day passes so slowly – she would say her prayers and go to bed. Late in the night the front door would slam; she could hear her mother's voice and laughter and the jingling spurs of the officer who accompanied her home. The noise of the spurs was like some pleasing music, a fanfare of silvery sounds that faded away into the distance; then she would fall asleep. Sometimes she would dream about the time, long ago, when she was a very little girl, when Mademoiselle Rose hadn't come yet; and if Mademoiselle Rose had gone into the kitchen to get a drink, leaving her alone in her room, she would wake up and call out in anguish, 'Mademoiselle Rose, are you there?'

A moment later a white light, a long nightdress with a white bodice would appear in the dark room. 'Of course I'm here.'

'Can I have a drink, please?'

Hélène would drink, then murmur, half asleep, carelessly pushing away the glass that she knew would be safe in the caring hands, 'You . . . you do love me, don't you?'

'Yes, I do. Go back to sleep.'

No kisses: Hélène hated them. No affection either, not in her gestures, not in the sound of her voice; Hélène scorned such things. But in the darkness that surrounded her she needed to hear those reassuring words, that warm tone of voice: 'Yes, I do. Go back to sleep.' She asked for nothing more. She breathed into her pillow and placed her cheek against the warm patch it had left, feeling peaceful, sinking into a calm forgetfulness.

# 4

Hélène walked beside Mademoiselle Rose, holding on to the Frenchwoman's sleeve and basking in the sweet warmth that spread from the scrap of material in her hand through her whole body. It was three o'clock on a winter's day. Night fell quickly at this time of year; lanterns were placed along the streets and they made the shops look mysterious, supernatural and a bit frightening, their little flames swaying beneath the shop signs: a rusty boot that creaked in the wind, a large golden loaf of bread with a thick crust made of ice, or an enormous pair of scissors, gaping half-open, ready to slice off a piece of the dark sky. Caretakers sat in the entranceways to buildings, shiny icicles hanging from their clothes. Both sides of the street were piled high with snow as tall as a man; it was hard, compact and sparkled beneath the flames of the lanterns.

They were going to visit the Grossmanns, whose children were friends of Hélène's. The Grossmanns were a wellestablished, wealthy, middle-class family and they despised Madame Karol. The housekeeper showed them in.

From the next room, they heard a woman's voice: 'Not all at once, my darlings,' she said, laughing. 'You're messing up my hair, you're killing me!' Then joyful children shouting, 'Mama! Mama!' Their voices rose and fell like the virtuoso scales that flow from one end of the keyboard to the other. Then came a man's voice: 'Come now, calm down; leave your mother in peace, my darlings . . .'

Hélène stood in silence, eyes lowered; Mademoiselle Rose took her hand and led her into the room.

The laughter stopped. The sitting room looked the same as the Karols'. It had the same golden torchère, the same black piano and velvet stool: all the newly married couples ordered these things while on honeymoon in Paris. But to Hélène everything seemed brighter and prettier than at home. In the middle of the room a woman was stretched out on a sofa upholstered in flowered fabric.

It was Madame Grossmann. Hélène knew her, but she had never seen her like this before, in a light-pink dressing gown with a tangle of children hanging from her arms. Her husband, a bald young man with a fat cigar in his mouth, was standing beside the sofa, leaning towards his wife; he looked bored to death and his eyes wandered a little impatiently from his family in front of him to the door, through which he would clearly have liked to escape. But Hélène wasn't looking at him; she was eagerly studying the young woman with her three children whose impatient little hands tugged at her dishevelled black hair; the youngest child, nestled in his mother's arm, gently nipped at her exposed cheek and neck like a little puppy.

'She isn't wearing any make-up,' Hélène thought bitterly.

The two older children sat at their mother's feet; the eldest girl was pale and sickly, her dark curls coiled round her ears, but the second-eldest had great pink cheeks that looked as if you could eat them; you could imagine them melting in your mouth when you kissed her, like ripe fruit.

'I don't have such beautiful cheeks,' thought Hélène. 'No, I don't.' Then she noticed Grossmann's face, his tense, controlled smile, his eyes fixed on the door. 'He's bored,' she mused with malicious satisfaction; sometimes, thanks to some mysterious power in her soul, she seemed able to sense the thoughts and feelings of others.

'Hélène, hello,' Madame Grossmann said sweetly.

She was a thin, unattractive woman, but with the liveliness and grace of a bird; there had been a slight note of pity in her voice.

Hélène lowered her head; her heavy fur-lined coat was making her feel unbearably hot; she paid little attention to the conversation going on above her head.

'I've brought a pattern for a collar for Nathalie . . .'

'Oh, Mademoiselle Rose, you are so very kind. Hélène can take off her coat and play with my girls for a bit, can't you, Hélène?'

'Oh, no! Thank you, Madame, but it's late . . .'

'Very well. Another time, then.'

The pink lamp cast such a soft, warm light . . . Hélène looked at the gossamer dressing gown, decorated with chiffon flounces; the three girls pressed against it, cocooned themselves into its fold, without being afraid of crumpling it. Their mother stroked the three dark heads, one after the other, as she spoke.

'They're all ugly,' Hélène thought in despair. 'They're all stupid. Clinging on to their mother's skirts as if they were babies, how shameful! And that Nathalie who's a head taller than me . . .'

Hélène looked at the children and they looked back in silence. Nathalie, who seemed to understand Hélène's discomfort and enjoy it, played hide and seek with her fat, malicious face, covering it with the folds of her mother's dressing gown and then, when she was sure her mother couldn't see her, coming out again to puff up her cheeks, stick out her tongue, squint and pull horrible faces, until Madame Grossmann looked towards her, when she suddenly put on the expression of a sweet, smiling, chubby-cheeked little angel.

'Monsieur Karol has gone away', Hélène heard someone say, 'for two years, I believe?'

'Working in the gold mines,' said Mademoiselle Rose.

'In Siberia, how awful . . .'

'He's not complaining; I think he likes the climate.'

'But two years away! The poor little girl . . .'

Mademoiselle Rose held Hélène's face close to her and stroked it. The child pulled away angrily. For the first time in her life she was ashamed of being abandoned: she didn't want these people to see her governess consoling her.

They left. Hélène now walked on ahead and every time Mademoiselle Rose took her hand, she slowly pulled away, not harshly, but with the sly determination of a dog who wishes to pull free from a lead that is annoying him. At the street corners a biting wind lashed her face, causing tears to well up in her eyes; she furtively wiped her nose and eyes with the end of her fur glove where little flakes of ice were beginning to form.

'Cover your mouth with your muff. Stand up straight, Hélène . . .'

She didn't take much notice; she stood up straight for a moment, then immediately dropped her head again. For the first time she thought seriously about her life and her family, but with a passionate attempt to find some sort of stability and happiness in her own existence; it was not in her nature to give in to pointless despair.

'I'm happy too when I'm in my room with the lamp on. We'll soon be home. I'll sit down at my little yellow desk . . .' She pictured with fondness the little desk of painted wood, which was just the right size for her, then the oil lamp with its green porcelain shade, shedding a milky light over her book. 'No, I won't read. All those books make me anxious and unhappy. I have to be happy; I have to be like other people. Tonight I'll have my glass of milk, my bread and jam, the last piece of chocolate before brushing my teeth. When no one is watching I'll hide the *Mémorial* under my pillow. No, no. Tonight, I'll cut out pictures, I'll draw . . . I'm happy; I want to be a happy little girl,' she thought. And the thick ice and sinister shadows beneath a nearby porch, the dark windows with melting snow flowing down them like tears, became a blur before her eyes, merging to form a black, restless sea.

# 5

When Hélène first began to understand life, Sunday became a day she anticipated with a feeling of sad anguish: Mademoiselle Rose spent every Sunday with some French friends, leaving Hélène hostage to the crushing affection of her elderly grandmother. Once she'd learned her lessons, nothing lightened the empty hours, nothing allowed her to take refuge in an alternative universe, one that was sweet and tinged with brilliant silver from the last rays of light before sunset, one that chimed like the porcelain cup that sat on the sideboard. On Sundays, as soon as she opened a book, her grandmother would groan, 'My darling, my sweet, sweet treasure, you're going to wear out your beautiful eyes . . .'

And if Hélène were playing, she'd say, 'Don't bend down so much. You'll hurt yourself. Don't jump. You'll fall. Don't throw your ball against the wall. You'll annoy Grandpa. Come and sit on my lap, my darling, let me hold you close to my heart . . .'

It was an old heart, one that to the youthful Hélène seemed

so cold and so slow to come to life. Yet it beat anxiously, passionately; those old eyes looked down in timid hope, trying to find something familiar on the child's face, an image, a distant memory . . .

'Oh! Grandma, let me go,' said Hélène.

If Hélène wasn't there, her grandmother did nothing for days on end; she folded her thin hands and laid them on her lap; they were dark and furrowed by age and the household chores she suddenly decided to do every now and then, finding a kind of humble pleasure in washing and ironing, and allowing herself to be shooed away by the cook. Her entire life was scarred by the marks of misfortune and unhappiness; she had experienced poverty, illness, the death of people she loved; her husband had cheated on her, betrayed her; she felt that her daughter and her husband could barely stand her. She had been born old, anxious, weary, while everyone around her was overflowing with vitality and passionate desires. But her main affliction was a kind of prophetic sadness; she seemed more inclined to fear the future than weep for the past. Her lamentations weighed heavily on her granddaughter; her foolish words caused Hélène to feel a rush of terror, terror that she felt lived deep within her heart, and which seemed to form part of some obscure legacy. Fear of being alone, fear of dying, fear of the dark and the dread that, on a day just like today, she might watch Mademoiselle Rose go out, never to return.

She had often heard her friends' mothers talking to Mademoiselle Rose with that hypocritically doting expression used when saying things children aren't meant to understand: 'If you were agreeable . . . We could go up to fifty roubles a month, or more. I've spoken to my husband about it. He's very willing. You are sacrificing yourself, dear Mademoiselle Rose, and for what? Children are ungrateful creatures . . .'

Life was unsettled, insecure, unstable. Nothing lasted. A merciless flood swept away peaceful days, the people you loved, carrying them far, far away, keeping you and them apart, for ever. A rush of anguish suddenly ran through the child, making her shudder; she sat in a corner holding a book, quiet and alone; she felt as if she could sense the solitude of the grave; the room became hostile and frightening; beyond the narrow circle of the light from the lamp, darkness reigned; the shadows slithered towards Hélène, rising to engulf her; she strained to push them away, like a swimmer pushing back the water with his arms. The sudden appearance of a pale ray of light beneath the door made her blood run cold. It was almost nightfall and Mademoiselle Rose wasn't there . . . would never be there again . . . 'She's not coming back. One day she'll disappear and I'll never see her again.'

No one would say anything to her. That's how they had once hidden the fact that her dog had died. To avoid her annoying them with tears they'd said, 'He's sick, but he'll be back . . .' adding the torment of hope to her sadness. The day Mademoiselle Rose left they'd do exactly the same; they wouldn't say a word to her; at suppertime she would be surrounded by lying faces: 'Eat. Go to bed. She's been held up. She'll be back.'

She could almost hear their hypocritical, pitying voices. She looked around her with hatred. Emptiness, silence, dismal tranquillity and the fear that cunningly digs at the heart to torture it – these were her only companions. She was forced to live with the anguish that flowed through her veins, to suffer it as if it were some hereditary evil; she could feel the weight of anxious terror heavy on her delicate bones, the same terror that had bowed the shoulders and drained the faces of so many of her race.

But when she was ten years old she began to find a melancholy charm in the solitude of these Sundays. She liked the extraordinary silence of those long, self-contained days, which were like faint little suns in a different universe where time flowed at a calmer pace.

Daylight spread slowly up the silk-lined walls, once the colour of wine but now moth-eaten and pink, faded by many summers. When the sun's rays reached the moulding, they became nothing more than a pale wash of light that slowly dissipated, leaving only the white, luminous ceiling to mirror the sky.

It was the very beginning of autumn; the air was clear and cold, and if you listened closely, you could hear the ice-cream seller's bell ringing as he drove down the avenue. In the courtyard the trees were almost bare, most of their leaves blown away by the August wind, when autumn is already starting in such climates – pared-down trees, decorated only at the top by dry leaves, pink with the sun that shone through them.

One day Hélène went into her mother's bedroom. She liked going in there. She had the vague feeling that, in this way, she could better take her mother by surprise, discover her secrets. She was beginning to become interested in her mother and in the mysterious life she now led entirely outside the house. She nurtured in her heart a strange hatred of her that seemed to increase as she grew older; like love, there were a thousand reasons for it and none; and, like love, there was the simple excuse: 'It's because of who she is, and because of who I am.'

She went into the room. She opened the drawers, played with her mother's costume jewellery, things bought in Paris that had been thrown untidily into the bottom of the wardrobe. From the next room her grandmother called out, 'What are you doing in there?'

'I'm looking for some clothes to dress up in,' said Hélène.

She was sitting on the rug, holding a nightdress she had found at the back of the chest of drawers.

The material was torn in several places; a heavy, strong hand had no doubt pulled at the lace shoulder strap so that it remained attached only by a few silk threads. It gave off a strange odour, a mixture of her mother's perfume, which she hated, the scent of tobacco and a richer, warmer smell, one she didn't recognise, but which she breathed in with amazement, with apprehension, with a kind of primitive sense of modesty. 'I hate how this smells,' she thought.

She raised the torn silk to her face a few times, each time pushing it away again. An amber necklace had been thrown into the back of a drawer; she took hold of it, touched it for a moment, then picked up the nightdress again and closed her eyes, the way one does when trying to recall some distant memory, long forgotten. But no, she couldn't remember anything; instead, her dormant, childlike sensuality rose up from deep within her for the very first time, making her feel anxious shame and ironic resentment. In the end she rolled the nightdress into a ball, threw it against the wall and trampled on it; then she walked out of the bedroom, but the scent lingered on her hands and pinafore. It stayed with her even as she slept, seeping into her childlike dreams, like a faraway call, like one note of music, like the husky, moaning cry of ringdoves in springtime.

# 6

The Manassé family, whose son was a friend of Hélène's, lived in a wooden house surrounded by a garden in an isolated part of the town. It was late autumn and the children were confined to the safety of their room, to protect them from the cold air that Russians feared as if it were a plague. That year, when Hélène came to play with the Manassé children on Sundays, their favourite game was to jump out of the schoolroom window, crawl along the sitting-room balcony and then jump down into the garden where the first snow had already fallen. Once there, they would throw snowballs at each other while playing at soldiers or highwaymen, dressed in old billowing capes, which they pretended were the romantic cloaks of warriors, and carrying branches – their wooden sabres and riding crops. The snow hadn't yet had a chance to freeze and go hard; it was moist and heavy, with the lingering bitter smell of rotting earth, of rain, of autumn.

The two little Manassé boys were chubby, pale, blond, lethargic and docile. Hélène sent them off to build a shelter out of branches and dried leaves in a corner of the shed while she remained huddled in the darkness of the balcony, silently observing what the Manassés and their friends were doing and saying inside. They were calmly playing cards beneath the lamplight, but in her imagination they symbolised the Russian and Austrian High Command on the eve of the Battle of Austerlitz. The Manassé boys were Napoleon's formidable army, barely visible in the distance; the hut they were building was a fortress: whoever took control of it would win the battle. Sitting in a circle round the green table, the Manassés were the perfect picture of the Austrian command bent over their maps and plans; she herself, outside in the darkness, in the snow and wind, was the brave young captain who had risked his life to cross the line of defence and penetrate the very heart of the enemy camp.

In this peaceful town, where books and newspapers were always abandoned half-finished, where no one ever dared bring politics into the conversation, while private matters were as tranquil and harmless as the calm waters of a river, flowing peacefully from honest mediocrity to honest simplicity, where people gave their blessing to adultery so that time transformed love affairs into a second, honourable marriage respected by everyone, including the husband – in this world, human passions were hidden behind playing cards and bitterly disputed small winnings. The days were short, the nights long; people spent their time playing cards, Whist or Whint, taking it in turns to go to each other's houses.

Madame Manassé was sitting on a wing-backed armchair; she was fat, with a face the colour of flour and hair dyed gold piled high on her head; her ample bosom fell over her stomach, which in turn rested on her knees; her chubby cheeks shook like jelly. On one side of her was her husband, who wore glasses and had cold, pale hands; on the other her long-standing lover, who was even older, fatter and balder than her husband. A young woman with dark hair worn up in a long roll above her forehead sat opposite the window. She chain-smoked and talked incessantly so that a thin stream of sweet-smelling smoke flowed from her nostrils, like the Oracle of Delphi in a trance. It was she who raised her head and noticed Hélène's pale face pressed against the window.

'How many times have we told those children not to go out in such weather,' said Madame Manassé, shaking her head reproachfully. She opened the window.

Hélène slipped through and jumped into the room. 'Don't scold your boys, Madame. They didn't want to disobey you; they stayed in their room,' she said, looking up at Madame Manassé with bright, innocent eyes. 'And as for me, well, I'm wrapped up warm and not afraid of the cold.'

'What am I going to do with these children!'

As soon as she had been reassured that her own children were safely inside, however, she just smiled and stretched out her hand – it smelled of almond soap – to feel Hélène's curls. 'What beautiful hair you have,' she said.

But because it really was too much for her to compliment Bella Karol's daughter she added, 'You hair's not naturally curly, is it?' Her lips were so pursed that the words came out in a kind of soft whistle, like the sound of a flute.

'Jealous bitch,' thought Hélène.

'Is your father going to be living in St Petersburg now?'

'I don't know, Madame.'

'She speaks French so well!' said Madame Manassé.

She continued to gently stroke Hélène's curls; her hands were pale and fat, and the curls straightened as they ran through her fingers. Every now and again she would raise her hands, gently shaking them to force the blood back down her long veins so her skin could retain its paleness. She pushed back Hélène's hair to reveal her ears, noted with a sigh of regret that they were small and well formed, then carefully arranged the curls over her forehead.

'Don't you find her French wonderful? She has no accent at all. Mademoiselle Rose is from Paris and it shows. She has good taste and nimble fingers. Your mama is lucky to have her. So you didn't know that your father was going to live in St Petersburg? And you as well, of course. Hasn't your mother told you anything?'

'No, Madame. Not yet . . .'

'She'll be happy to see your father after so many years. Ah, how she must be looking forward to that. If I had to be apart from my darling husband . . . well, I can't even imagine it,' said Madame Manassé with feeling. 'But not everyone has the same nature, thank goodness. It's been two years, hasn't it? Two years since your father left?'

'Yes, Madame.'

'Two years . . . You still remember him, I hope?'

'Oh, yes, Madame.'

Did she remember her father? 'Of course,' thought Hélène; her heart ached when she thought of him, recalling exactly how he looked when he used to come into her room each evening . . . 'Yet this is the first time I've thought about him since he left,' mused Hélène, her heart full of affection and remorse.

'Mama isn't too bored, is she?' asked Madame Manassé.

Hélène coldly studied the faces all around her, each one tense with eager curiosity. The young woman's nostrils trembled, releasing blue rings into the air. The men looked at each other and sniggered, saying 'hm' while tapping their dry, gnarled fingers on the table; they sighed, shrugged their shoulders and glanced at Hélène with irony and pity in their eyes.

'No, she's not bored . . .'

'Ah hah!' said one of the men, laughing. 'Out of the mouths of babes, as they say. I knew your mother when she was barely older than you, Mademoiselle.'

'Did you also know Safronov senior when he was at the height of his success?' asked Madame Manassé. 'When I came to live here he was already old.'

'Yes, I did know him. He squandered three fortunes: his mother's, his wife's and his daughter's, who had some money left to her by his wife's father. Three fortunes . . .'

'Quite apart from his own, I imagine.'

'He never had a penny, which didn't stop him from living the high life, I can assure you. As for Bella, she was just a schoolgirl when I first met her . . .'

Hélène thought of the photograph of her mother when she was a child: she'd been a chubby girl with a round face and hair worn up, with a comb to hold it in place. But she dismissed this image at once: to think that the mother she so feared and hated had once been a little girl like any other, that even *she* had the right to reproach her parents, would allow too many subtleties to seep into the cruel picture of her mother that Hélène had long ago secretly etched into her heart.

'Hélène has beautiful eyes,' murmured Madame Manassé.

'She looks like her father; there's no doubt about it!' someone said disappointedly.

'Oh, my dear . . .'

'What! These things happen. But I know a particular person who has always been lucky . . .'

'Ivan Ivanitch, you terrible gossip, stop it right now!' said Madame Manassé. She laughed and glanced sideways towards Hélène as if to say, 'The child will understand . . . It's not her fault . . .'

'How old are you, Hélène?'

'Ten, Madame.'

'She's a big girl now. Her mother will soon start thinking about finding a husband.'

'She won't have any trouble doing that. Did you know that the way things are going, Karol will soon be a millionaire?'

'Now, let's not exaggerate!' said Madame Manassé; she suddenly found it difficult to speak, as if the words burned her mouth as she spoke them. 'He has earned a lot of money, or so they say. Some people think he's discovered a new mine, which, by the way, strikes me as the most likely, but others say he's improved the output of the old one. It's possible. I have no idea. There are so many ways to make a fortune for a man who's . . . clever . . . But whatever the case may be, money earned quickly gets spent quickly, my dears. Rushing all over the world is not always the best way to get rich. Although Lord knows I wish him all the prosperity in the world, the poor man . . .'

'You know what they say: "Luck of the . . ."'

'Come now, do be quiet. You're as bad as some gossipy old woman. Don't judge and you won't be judged,' said Madame Manassé. She pulled Hélène to her bosom and kissed her.

Hélène was repulsed; she felt as if she were drowning between those warm, heavy, quivering breasts. 'May I go and play now, Madame?'

'Of course you can. Run off and play, my darling Hélène; have a really wonderful time while you're here, my poor dear. Look at how nicely she does her curtsey. She's such a charming little girl . . .'

Hélène ran back out into the garden where the boys greeted her with shouts of joy, wild gestures and by pulling faces, just as children do when they are overexcited and tired at the end of the weekend.

'Forward march!' she said swiftly. 'To the right! Battle formation!'

The autumn snow sprinkled a shiny, dry, white powder over them in the early night. Carrying a stick over her shoulder, her long cape billowing behind her, Hélène led the weary, shivering, panting boys around the bushes and through the woods, delighting in the feel of the wind and the damp, bitter smell of the air.

But her heart felt heavy in her chest, weighed down by an inexplicable pain.

# 7

In summer, when it started getting hot, Hélène would go out
to play in the public gardens. The air was thick with dust
and smelled of dung and roses. As soon as they crossed the
avenue the noise of the city faded away; here the street was
bordered with gardens and old, sprawling lime trees; the
houses were barely visible at the end of the pathways; every
now and again you could just make out through the branches
the pink walls of a little church or a golden clock tower.
There were never any cars and few passers-by. The leaves
that had fallen to the ground muffled the sound of footsteps.
Hélène ran on ahead, happy, impatient, always circling back
to Mademoiselle Rose in the thousand ways children and
dogs do when out for a walk. She felt free, joyful and strong.
She wore a white broderie anglaise dress with three layers,
a silk belt, and two large, delicate wide bows, securely fixed
by two pins to the outer skirt of starched taffeta, a straw
hat with lace trim, a white bow in her hair, patent leather
shoes and black silk socks. In spite of this, she managed to
run and jump and climb on to every bench, crushing and

scattering the green leaves, while Mademoiselle Rose said, 'You're going to tear your dress, Lili . . .'

But she wasn't listening. She was ten years old; she felt the harsh, intense joy of being alive with a kind of intoxicating satisfaction.

Opposite the public gardens was a short, steep street, and where old women sold strawberries and miniature roses; they were hunched over and barefoot in the dust, their hair covered by white kerchiefs to protect them from the sun; hard, green little apples sat in buckets full of water.

Processions of pilgrims often passed along the road, on their way to the famous Dnieper monasteries. Their arrival was heralded by a horrible stench of filth and open wounds; singing hymns at the top of their voices, they marched past, followed by a cloud of yellow dust. The pale, translucent flowers from the lime trees fell on to their bare heads and clung to their bushy beards. The obese prelates, with their long, straight, dark hair, held up heavy gold icons that shot beams of fire when struck by the bright sun. The dust, the military music coming from the park, the shouts of the pilgrims, the sunflower seeds swirling in the air, all created the atmosphere of a wild, drunken party that entranced Hélène, making her head spin so she felt mildly queasy.

'Come on, now, quickly!' said Mademoiselle Rose, taking the child by the hand and pulling her along. 'They're dirty . . . they're bringing all sorts of diseases with them. Come on, Hélène!'

Every year, during the same period, soon after the pilgrims arrived, epidemics raged through the city. The children suffered most. The year before, the Grossmanns' eldest daughter had died.

Hélène obeyed and ran on ahead, but for a long time she heard the echo of the chants carried by the wind as they faded away into the distance towards the Dnieper.

In the park the military band of brass instruments and drums played at full blast while university students circled slowly round the fountain one way, and the secondary school students linked arms and circled in the opposite direction. High above the crowd, sunbeams struck the statue of Emperor Nicholas I, sending out brilliant rays of light.

All the students smiled as they passed each other, whispering and exchanging flowers, love letters, promises. The flirting, the game-playing went right over Hélène's head; not that she was ignorant of them, but she wasn't yet curious about 'that', as she scornfully called it to herself.

'How stupid they look the way they wink and giggle and shriek!'

Games, races with the other children, she was happy doing those things. Was there any pleasure equal to running, her hair whipping her face, her cheeks burning like two flames, her heart pounding? The breathlessness, the wild spinning of the park around her, the shouts she let out almost without noticing, what pleasures could compete with those?

Faster, ever faster . . . They bumped into the legs of passers-by, slipped near the edge of the fountain, fell on to the soft, cool grass . . .

It was forbidden to go down the dark paths where couples kissed on benches in the shadows. Yet Hélène and the boys she played with always ended up there, racing on ahead; their indifferent childlike eyes saw, without really seeing, pale faces glued to one another, held in place by two soft, quivering mouths.

One day – it was the summer she turned ten – Hélène jumped over the railings on to one of these paths – tearing the lace of her dress as she did so – and hid in the grass; on a bench opposite her two young lovers were embracing; the fairground music that filled the gardens faded away as night fell; there was only a distant, delightful murmur: the sound of water flowing from the fountain, of birds singing and muffled voices. The sun's rays could not penetrate the vault created by the oaks and lime trees; lying on her back and looking up, Hélène watched the early evening light as it shimmered at the tops of the trees; it was six o'clock. Sweat ran down her burning face and was dried by the wind, leaving her skin feeling soft and cool; she closed her eyes. The boys could look for her . . . She was bored by them . . . Golden, translucent insects flew down, perching on the tall grass; she enjoyed blowing gently on their motionless wings: they would slowly unfold, then let the wind lift them upwards to disappear into the blue sky. She imagined she was helping them fly. She loved to roll around in the grass, to feel it beneath her warm little palms, to rub her cheek against the fragrant earth. Through the railings, she could see the wide, empty street. A dog sat on the stony ground licking its wounds, groaning and howling loudly; church bells rang softly, lazily; some time later a lone group of weary pilgrims passed by; they were no longer singing but walked silently through the dust in their bare feet while the ribbons from the icon they were holding out in front of them barely billowed in the calm air.

On the bench sat a young girl; she was wearing the uniform of the town's secondary school: brown dress, black smock, hair pulled back in a little round bun beneath a straw hat;

Posnansky, the son of a Polish lawyer, was kissing her in silence.

'She's a fool,' mused Hélène. She looked mockingly at the pink cheeks that turned fiery scarlet beneath the girl's coil of black hair.

Like a conqueror, the boy threw off his grey schoolboy's cap, decorated with the Imperial eagle. 'You have really silly ideas, Tonia, if you don't mind me saying so,' he said in his uneven, hoarse young boy's voice that was starting to change; it still had some of the soft, feminine intonation of a child.

'If you like,' he said, 'we could go to the edge of the Dnieper tonight, in the moonlight. If you only knew how nice it is. You light a big fire on the grass and lie down. It's as comfortable as a bed and you can hear the nightingales singing . . .'

'Oh, do be quiet!' murmured the young girl, blushing as she weakly pushed away the hands that were unbuttoning her blouse. 'Absolutely not. If my family found out . . . and I'm afraid; I don't want you to look down on me. You boys are all the same . . .'

'*Chérie!*' said the boy, pulling her face towards his.

'Poor little fool,' thought Hélène. 'What kind of pleasure or enjoyment could she possibly get out of rubbing her cheek against those hard metal buttons, or feeling the rough material of his uniform against her chest, or his mouth, dripping wet no doubt, against hers . . . ugh . . . Is *that* what they call love?'

The boy's impatient hand pulled the shoulder strap of the schoolgirl's smock so hard that the material gave way; Hélène saw two little breasts emerge; they were barely formed, tender and white, grasped by the eager fingers of her sweetheart. 'How horrible!' she whispered.

She quickly looked away, buried herself deep in the gently billowing grass, for the wind had risen as night fell; the breeze held the scent of the nearby river and the rushes and reeds that lined it. For a moment she imagined the slow-moving river beneath the moon, the fires lit along its banks. The year she'd had whooping cough, the doctor had recommended a change of air, so her father had taken her on boat rides, sometimes at dusk after he got home from the office. They would stop for the night in one of the white monasteries dotted across the little islands. That was so long ago . . . Her thoughts drifted to how different her house had seemed back then, more like everyone else's, more 'normal' . . . She tried to find another word to describe it, but in vain.

'. . . More normal . . . They used to fight, but . . . it wasn't the same . . . Everyone fights . . . whereas now, *she's* never there . . . Where on earth could she be going, I wonder, all night long?'

As she followed her train of thought, she remembered that her mother sometimes talked about the Dnieper at night and how the nightingales sang in the old lime trees along the riverbank . . .

She started whistling, picking up the fallen branch of a tree that lay on the grass and slowly peeling off the bark.

'The Dnieper in the moonlight, at night . . . Love, people in love,' she murmured. 'Love.' She hesitated for a moment and quietly spoke the word her mother sighed when reading French romantic novels: 'Lover . . . A lover, that's what it's called . . .'

Yet there was something else she was trying hard to remember and couldn't, something that made her feel uneasy . . . But it was time to go home; the first jets of water from the sprinklers sprayed on to the lilacs, and their strong, powerful scent rose into the air. She stood up and walked past the bench, with her head turned in the other direction.

But in spite of herself, as soon as she had reached the end of the path she secretly glanced back at the amorous couple with a vague feeling of repulsion, shame and fascination; their silent kiss was so long and sweet that for a second a feeling of painful tenderness shot through her like an arrow. She shrugged her shoulders and, like an indulgent old woman, thought, 'Let them get on with it if it makes them happy.'

She climbed over the railings, undeterred by the brambles that covered them and scratched her calves, and took the long way back to the place where Mademoiselle Rose sat finishing some Irish embroidery on a collar.

They went home; Hélène was silent, resting her head against Mademoiselle Rose. In the dusk, you could still clearly see the statue of Nicholas I on his pedestal, his silent face menacing above the drowsy city; but the streets were now nothing more than fragrant shadowy shapes full of whispers, the last sleepy chirping of birds, the pale silhouettes of bats against the moon, the beautiful round, pink moon . . .

At this time of day the house was empty. 'She' was roaming about, Lord knows where. Her grandfather was eating an ice cream on the terrace of the Café François, thinking with nostalgia of Paris and the Café Tortoni. The fragrant ice cream melted in the heat of the early night air.

The French newspapers he was reading flapped merrily on their poles in the light wind. Hélène may not have been thinking about him, but he was thinking about her with kindness and affection. She was the only one in the world he loved. Bella was egotistical, a bad mother. 'As for her behaviour, well, that's nothing to do with me any more, thank the Lord. Besides, she's right: the only good thing in life is love. But the little girl . . . She's so intelligent. The child will suffer . . . she already understands, she can sense it.' Ah, well. What could he do about it? He hated confrontations, lectures, quarrels . . .

At his age he deserved to be left in peace. And then there was the money, the money . . . The money didn't belong to Bella, but she knew only too well how to make sure he didn't forget that it was thanks to her and her husband they were able to survive. And she always reminded him of how he'd squandered his fortune. His darling daughter . . . And yet, she loved him; she was proud of him, of how young he still looked, of his fine clothes, of his perfect French accent. They got along rather well living together, without annoying each other, without spying on each other. Everything will work out eventually. She'll get older. She'll be like the other women, keeping herself busy with gossip and card games, and she might even develop some affection for her daughter . . .

Anything was possible. Nothing was really that important. He ordered one last pistachio ice cream and ate it slowly to savour it, looking up at the stars.

Back at home, Hélène's grandmother was pacing back and forth between the windows: 'Hélène . . . Hélène isn't home yet. It rained this morning. But Mademoiselle Rose is bringing her up like a French child . . . French,' she thought with hatred. 'Exposing the child to risks with open windows and draughts . . .'

Oh, how she hated Mademoiselle Rose. It was a shy hatred, but a profound one. It filled her heart, yet she hid it even from herself, thinking only, 'They couldn't possibly love the child like we do, those governesses, those foreigners . . .'

Hélène walked in silence; she was thirsty. She thought longingly of the taste of the cold milk that was waiting for her in the old blue bowl that sat on the washstand in her bedroom. How she would throw back her head and drink it, how she would feel the sweet, icy milk flow past her lips and run down her throat . . . She even imagined the brilliant moon shining behind the windowpane, as if its cool light added even more to the delicious sensation of satisfied thirst.

Then, suddenly, when she was nearly home, she remembered the nightdress she'd discovered in her mother's bedroom, the nightdress, torn like the schoolgirl's black smock . . . She let out a little 'ah' of surprise, experiencing the intense pleasure of intellectual satisfaction at understanding something; she grabbed Mademoiselle Rose's hand and smiled, staring up at her with an intense, malicious expression in her brown eyes. 'I understand now,' she said. '*She* has lovers, doesn't she?'

'Be quiet, Hélène, be quiet,' whispered Mademoiselle Rose.

But Hélène thought to herself, 'She knew who I meant right away.'

She let out a happy, birdlike little cry, jumped up on to an old stone boundary marker while cooing, 'A lover . . . a lover!

She has a lover!' Then, suddenly weary and seeing the lamp being lit in her room, she remembered how thirsty she was. 'Oh, Mademoiselle Rose, dearest Mademoiselle Rose,' she said. 'Why aren't I allowed to eat ice cream?'

But Mademoiselle Rose was lost in thought and so said nothing.

# 8

Hélène's life, like everyone else's, had its own haven of
light. Every year she returned to France with her mother
and Mademoiselle Rose. How happy she was to see Paris
again. She loved it so much. Now that Karol was getting
rich, his wife stayed at the Grand Hotel in Paris, but Hélène
stayed in a grim, sordid little guest house behind Notre-
Dame-de-Lorette. Hélène was growing up; it was necessary
to keep her as far away as possible from the life her
mother enjoyed. Madame Karol paid for Hélène's and
Mademoiselle Rose's accommodation out of her personal
allowance, thus reconciling her own self-interest with the
demands of morality. But Hélène was perfectly happy. For
a few months she could mingle with French children of
her own age.

How she envied them! She never grew tired of studying
them. To be born in these ordinary, peaceful neighbourhoods
where all the houses looked alike – how wonderful that would
be. To be born and grow up here. To have Paris as her home.
Not to have to see her mother every morning when they met

at the Bois de Boulogne, walking slowly beside her down the Allée des Acacias (and having fulfilled this duty, Bella Karol believed she had done what was necessary and had no need to think about her daughter until the next day, unless she fell seriously ill), not to see her mother, with her Irish tweed jacket, her polka-dot veil, her skirt sweeping across the dead leaves, as she walked with all the plumed aplomb of, according to the popular expression of the day, a 'horse pulling a hearse' to meet an Argentinian with cigar-coloured skin. Not to have to travel by train for five days to return to a barbaric country where she didn't really feel at home either, because she spoke French better than Russian, because her hair was done in curls rather than tightly pulled back into shiny little plaits, because her dresses were based on Parisian fashion . . . Even, if necessary, to be the daughter of one of the shopkeepers near the Gare de Lyon. To wear a black smock and have cheeks as pink as radishes. To be able to ask her mother (a different mother), 'Mama, where are the penny notebooks?'

To be that little girl . . .

'Hélène, stand up straight.'

'Oh, damn!'

To be called Jeanne Fournier or Loulou Massard or Henriette Durand, a name that was easy to understand, easy to remember . . . But no. She wasn't like the others. Not completely. It was such a shame! And yet . . . She had a richer and fuller life than other children. She had experienced so many things. She had seen so many different places. She sometimes felt that two distinct souls inhabited her body. She was only a little girl, yet she already had so many memories that she had no trouble understanding that word that grown-ups used: 'experience'. Sometimes, when she thought about this, she was filled with an intoxicating feeling of joy. She would walk around Paris in the pinkish dusk, at six o'clock in the evening, when a flood of light filtered down on to the streets; she would hold Mademoiselle Rose's hand and look at all the faces as they passed by, imagining for each one of them a name, a past, their different loves and hates. She would think with pride: 'In Russia, they wouldn't understand the native language. They wouldn't understand the thoughts of a merchant or a coachman or a farmer. But *I* know. And, what's more, I understand *them* too. They may push me. They may kick my ball out of the way. They may think, "What a pain these little girls are." But I'm craftier than they are. Even though I'm a little girl, I've seen more things than they have in all their long, boring lives.'

She was thinking all this when she saw the Christmas displays in the windows of one of the biggest department stores. Once again, she imagined with yearning a Parisian family, a little apartment and a Christmas tree beneath a porcelain light hanging from the ceiling . . .

She was growing up. Her body was losing the stocky robustness of early childhood; her arms and legs were becoming lanky and thinner; her face was paler; her chin was longer and her eyes deeper; the beautiful pink blush in her cheeks was fading.

She spent the winter before the war in Nice, where she turned twelve. It was here that her father would appear, one day, back from Siberia to collect his family and take them to live with him in St Petersburg.

In Nice that year, Hélène listened for the first time to the gentle, loving sound of the sea, to romantic Italian songs and to the words 'love' and 'lover' without feeling indifferent scorn. The nights were so warm, smelled so sweet . . . She had reached the age when little girls suddenly come to life, their hearts pound and they press trembling hands to their flat chests beneath their ruffled blouses and think, 'In this many years I'll be fifteen, then sixteen . . . In this many years I'll be a woman . . .'

Boris Karol arrived one March morning. Later on, when she thought of her father, she would always think of his face as it looked that day, amid the smoke and bustle of the train station. He was stronger, with a swarthy complexion and red lips. When he bent down so she could kiss him, and she felt his rough cheek against her mouth, the feeling of love she suddenly felt for him filled her heart with a kind of joy that was so piercing it almost hurt. She walked away from Mademoiselle Rose and took her father's hand. He smiled down at her. When he laughed, his face lit up with fiery intelligence and a sort of mischievous cheerfulness. She affectionately kissed his beautiful tanned hand with its hard nails, just like hers. At that moment she heard a sad, shrill whistle from a train that was leaving, the leitmotif that, from then on, would always accompany the brief appearances her father made in her life. At the same time a conversation began that went over her head, a conversation that no longer sounded like human speech – for words were replaced by numbers – and one which would never cease to echo around her, above her, from now until death closed her father's lips.

'Millions, millions, stocks . . . shares in the Shell Bank

. . . shares in De Beers, bought at 25 and sold at 90 . . .'

A young girl walked slowly by, swaying her hips, a basket full of silvery fish balanced on her head: '*Sardini! Belli sardini!*' Her shrill voice made the 'i' sound as piercing as a seagull's cry.

'. . . I speculated . . . He speculated . . .'

The little bells on the carriage they'd hired jingled sweetly; the horse shook his long ears in the bag of straw; the coachman chewed on a flower.

'. . . I won . . . I lost . . . I won it back . . . Money, shares . . . Copper, silver mines, gold mines . . . phosphates . . . millions, millions, millions . . .'

Later on, after Karol had eaten lunch and changed his clothes, Hélène was allowed to go with him when he went out. They walked along the Promenade des Anglais. They said nothing. What could they have talked about? The only things that interested Karol were money, business, material things, and Hélène was an innocent child. She looked at him adoringly.

He smiled at her and pinched her cheek. 'Tell me, how would you like to go and have dinner in Monte Carlo?'

'Oh, yes!' Hélène said sweetly, half closing her eyes; she knew no better way to express her pleasure.

In Monte Carlo, after they'd had dinner, Karol seemed anxious. He tapped on the table for a moment, seemed to hesitate, then he suddenly got up and led her out.

They went into the casino. 'Wait for me here,' he said, pointing to the lobby; then he disappeared.

She sat down, being very careful to sit up straight and not to get her coat or gloves dirty. A haggard, tired woman stood in front of the mirror, smearing lipstick over her mouth; behind her, Hélène could see her own reflection: a small, thin little girl with curls all round her face, wearing her first real fur round her neck, a small ermine stole her father had brought back for her from Siberia. She waited for a long time. The hours passed. Men went inside, others came out. She saw strange faces, old women carrying shopping bags, their hands still trembling from having handled gold. This wasn't the first casino she'd ever seen; one of her earliest memories was having walked across the gambling rooms in Ostend, where players ignored the pieces of gold that sometimes rolled beneath their feet. But now she understood how to see beyond the superficial world. She looked at the women plastered in make-up and thought, 'Do they have children? Were they ever young? Are they happy?'

For there comes a time in life when the pity previously reserved only for other children takes on a different form, a time when we study the faces of 'old people' and sense that one day we will be just like them. And that is the moment when early childhood comes to an end.

Outside, it was getting dark; the sky was a beautiful velvet colour with luminous fountains, sweet smells, magnolias in blossom, a soft, caressing wind. Hélène looked out of the window, pressing her face against the glass panes; it was a night that seemed too intense, too sensual. 'Not for children,' she thought with a smile. She felt small, lost, guilty. (Why? I won't get caught. It's not my fault. I was with Papa. He wasn't with me for long, though . . .) It was eight o'clock in the evening. Some cars stopped in front of the Café de Paris; men in tuxedos got out, women in ball gowns. Beneath a balcony she could hear the sound of mandolins, kisses, muffled laughter. On the roads near the harbour dim lights cast shadows along the streets and all the cranes from the coastline converged, making their way towards the casino.

It was nine o'clock now . . . 'I'm hungry,' thought Hélène. 'What can I do? I just have to stay here; they won't let me into the gaming rooms.' How many people like her were waiting reluctantly? The entrance hall was full of anxious, tired women who waited patiently, without complaining. She felt strangely old and resigned, resigned to spend the night right there on the bench if she had to. If only her eyes wouldn't keep closing beneath her heavy eyelids. Time was passing so slowly . . . yet the hands of the clock on the Casino wall moved strangely quickly. It was nine-thirty just a little while ago, the time when she normally went to bed. But now the hands of the clock had moved forward, nine-forty-five, ten o'clock . . . To stop herself from falling asleep, she began pacing back and forth. A woman was coming and going in the darkness, waving a pink feather boa. Hélène looked at her. She felt that her mind was clearer because she was hungry; it mysteriously allowed her to see deep into the life of this nameless woman to such an extent that she could feel the woman's weariness and anxiety within her own soul. She was so hungry . . . She breathed in the smell of soup that was being brought upstairs in a tureen from the kitchens of the Café de Paris.

'I feel like a suitcase forgotten at the left luggage office,' she thought, trying to make fun of herself.

Obviously this was all so comical, so very comical . . . She looked around her. There were no other children: they were all asleep in bed. A caring hand had closed the windows and curtains. They couldn't hear the mumblings of the old man accosting the shop girls; they couldn't see the couples kissing on park benches.

'Mademoiselle Rose wouldn't have forgotten all about me, not Mademoiselle Rose. It's obvious that I'm still deluding myself,' she thought bitterly. 'She's the only one in the world who loves me . . .'

Eleven o'clock. In the moonlight the city looked pale, weary, strange, as in a dream . . . Hélène walked and walked, her eyes half closed with exhaustion, counting the lights in the houses along the harbour to prevent herself from falling asleep. Really, now! She mustn't whine. Was she going to start crying like some child left behind in a park? Now the last few horrid-looking women were coming out of the Casino, clutching their bags to their bosoms, their make-up melting down their faces. And behind them? Her father: his white hair, his features lit up with the inner flame of joy and passion she so admired.

He took her hand and squeezed it hard. 'My poor darling, come along. I'd forgotten about you. Let's go home right away.'

She didn't dare tell him she was hungry. She didn't want to see him shrug his shoulders and say with a sigh, as her mother would have done, 'Children . . . they're such a burden!'

'Did you at least win, Papa?'

Her father's lips trembled with a little smile that was both joyful and sad. 'Win? Yes, a little. But do people gamble in order to win?'

'Oh? Well, why else, then?'

'Just for the pleasure of playing, my girl,' said her father and the passionate blood that coursed through his veins seemed to flow hotly into Hélène's hand; he looked at her with affectionate scorn. 'You wouldn't understand. You're too young. And you'll never understand. You're just a woman.'

# PART II

# 1

One evening in the autumn of 1914, Hélène, Mademoiselle Rose and the last of their luggage arrived in St Petersburg, where Hélène's parents had already been living for several weeks.

As always, whenever Hélène had to see her mother again after a long absence, she trembled with apprehension, but she would have rather died than show it.

It was a particularly dismal, damp day in that sad season when there is hardly any sun, when you wake up, get up, eat and work by lamplight, and when soft, damp snow falls from a yellowish sky and is whipped away by a furious wind. How harshly it blew, that day, the biting north wind, and what a sickly odour of filthy water rose from the Neva.

The lights were lit along the streets. A thick fog wafted through the air like smoke. Hélène hated this strange city before she even arrived; now that she saw it, her heart ached as if something terrible was about to happen; she grasped Mademoiselle Rose's coat nervously, trying to find the familiar warmth of her hand, then turned round and studied

73

her reflection in the carriage window with sad surprise: it was tense and pale.

'What's the matter, Lili?' asked Mademoiselle Rose.

'Nothing. I'm cold. This city is horrible,' Hélène murmured in despair. 'And in Paris, the trees are all golden now.'

'But we couldn't have gone to Paris anyway, my poor little Hélène, because of the war,' Mademoiselle Rose said sadly.

They fell silent; heavy drops of rain fell swiftly down the windows, like tears down someone's face.

'*She* didn't even come to meet us at the station,' Hélène said bitterly; she felt a wave of sadness and venom rise up through her soul, emerging from immeasurable depths, from a part of her being that was alien to her.

'You mustn't call her "she" like that,' Mademoiselle Rose corrected her. 'You should say "Mama". "Mama didn't come to meet us" . . .'

'Mama didn't come to meet us. She probably doesn't want to see me that much,' said Hélène quietly. 'And I don't want to see her either.'

'Well, then, what are you complaining about?' Mademoiselle Rose replied softly. 'You've got a few more moments of peace.'

Hélène was struck by the mournful irony of her smile.

'Do *they* have a car now?' the little girl asked.

'Yes. Your father has earned a lot of money.'

'Really? And what about my grandparents? Will they ever come to live here?'

'I don't know.'

But Hélène knew very well that her grandparents would never leave the Ukraine; a regular allowance would keep them away from the Karols for ever. That was the very first thing Bella would do with her fortune.

When Hélène thought about her grandparents she felt pity, which she hated because it seemed cowardly to her. She tried to put them out of her mind, but in spite of herself, their faces surged up in her memory. She remembered them running quickly, stumbling along the platform as the train was leaving. Her grandmother was crying, which hardly made her look any different, the poor woman; but grandfather Safronov remained his usual swaggering self as he stood tall, waving his cane. 'See you soon,' he cried, his voice shaking. 'We'll come to see you in St Petersburg! Tell your mama to invite us soon.'

'I wouldn't count on it, poor Grandfather,' murmured Hélène. She was certain the old man understood the situation even better than she did. She couldn't imagine the fury and regret he would feel when going back home to the empty house, followed by his wife who moaned and wept quietly.

'It's my turn now,' he would think. 'My turn. Once I was the one who ran off to follow my whims, to enjoy myself, and left everyone behind. But now that I'm old and running out of steam, I'm the one who's being left behind.' And turning towards his wife, he deigned to wait for her for the first time in his life, even though he banged his cane against the ground and grumbled, 'Come on, then, hurry up, slow coach!'

'Exeunt' grandfather and grandmother, Hélène thought with the dark sense of humour she'd inherited from her father.

Meanwhile, the car had stopped in front of a large, beautiful house. The Karols' apartment was constructed in such a way that you could see right through all the rooms from the entrance hall; from the large open doors stretched a series of gold-and-white reception rooms. Hélène bumped into the corner of an enormous white piano, caught sight of her pale, confused face reflected in the many mirrors and finally made her way into a smaller, darker room to her mother. She was standing up, leaning against a table; beside her sat a young man whom Hélène had never seen before.

'Stuffed into a corset at three o'clock in the afternoon,' thought Hélène, remembering her mother's loose-fitting dressing gowns and dishevelled hair; she looked up and immediately spotted how many new rings she wore on her pale fingers, saw the elegant dress, her slim figure, how happy and passionate her harsh face looked; she saw all of it, enclosed it within her heart and never, ever forgot it.

'Hello, Hélène. Was the train early, then? I wasn't expecting you so soon.'

'Hello, Mama,' Hélène murmured.

She could never clearly pronounce both syllables whenever she said 'Mama'; she had difficulty getting the word out through her pursed lips; she said the last syllable with a kind of quick groan that she wrenched from her heart.

'Hello.'

The painted cheek lowered itself to her level; she kissed it carefully, instinctively trying to find a spot that wasn't covered in powder or rouge.

'Don't mess up my hair. Aren't you going to say hello to your cousin? Don't you recognise your cousin, Max Safronov?'

A smile of triumph passed over Bella's painted mouth, which was as thin and red as a trickle of blood.

Hélène suddenly remembered Lydia Safronov's horse-drawn carriage, which she sometimes came across on the streets of the town where she'd been born; she pictured the stiff woman with her little serpent's head poking out of the fur stole she wore, recalled her dark eyes and the cold way she looked at her.

'Max, here? Oh, they really *must* be very rich,' she thought.

She was fascinated by how pale the young man looked; it was the first time she'd ever seen the pale skin common to the inhabitants of St Petersburg, skin that seemed to have no blood at all, as pallid as a flower growing in a cave. He had a haughty, affected manner, a slim, delicate nose slightly curved into an eagle's beak, wide green eyes and blond hair that was already receding towards his temples, even though he was barely twenty-four years old.

He lightly stroked Hélène's cheek with one finger, then pinched her upraised chin. 'Hello, my little cousin. How old are you now?' he asked, clearly not knowing what he should say to her and staring at her with his bright, mocking green eyes.

He didn't listen to the reply.

'Look at how she stoops,' he murmured. 'You should stand up straight, my girl. When my sisters were your age they were a head taller than you and stood up as straight as an arrow.'

'It's true,' cried Bella, annoyed, 'just look at your posture! You should scold her, Mademoiselle Rose.'

'The journey has worn her out.'

'You always make excuses for her,' said Bella, irritated.

She slapped Hélène between her slim shoulder blades as soon as they slumped. 'You're not making yourself look any more attractive, my poor girl. No matter how often you scold

77

her, she simply won't listen. And see how sickly she looks, Max. Your sisters seem so athletic, so strong.'

'*It's the English education, you know*,' Max murmured in English. '*Cold baths and bare knees and not encouraged to feel sorry for themselves.* She doesn't look like you, Bella.'

'How's Papa?' asked Hélène.

'Well, Papa is fine; he came home very late, so you'll see him before you go to bed; he's very busy.'

They said no more. Hélène stood as stiff and straight as if she were in a parade, not daring to leave or sit down.

'All right, then,' Bella finally whispered, sounding weary and annoyed. 'Don't just stand there staring at me with your mouth hanging open. Go to your room; go and see your bedroom . . .'

Hélène went out, wondering with anguish what this stranger would bring her, happiness or misery, for she knew very well that from that moment on he would be the true master in her life. Later on, when she had grown up and remembered the way her mother's face leaned towards his, their silence, her mother's smile, everything she had noticed, guessed, sensed in a single look, she would sometimes think, 'It's impossible . . . I was only twelve, after all. The truth is that I came to understand gradually and now I've convinced myself that I saw everything in a flash. I understood what was happening little by little, and not in the space of an instant. I was a child and they didn't say anything that day; they weren't even sitting close to each other . . .' And yet whenever a colour, a sound, a scent took her back to the past, whenever she managed to remember the exact shape of Max's face when he was young, she immediately felt her child's soul rise up within her, as if awakened after a long sleep, whispering, passionately calling to her: 'You also cast your childhood aside! Don't you remember how you had the body of a young girl but a heart as old, as mature as it is today? So I clearly had good reason to feel sorry for myself: you had abandoned me, and even now you have forgotten all about me . . .'

On that day, that sad day, she knew for certain they were having an affair; she had feared for herself; she had immediately hated that scornful young man who had said, 'She doesn't look like you, Bella.'

'What about Papa? I'm only thinking about myself, I'm so self-centred. He must be suffering, if he knows . . .' she thought, and at once a bitter feeling filled her heart.

'Well, then, if no one really cares about me I'm going to have to love myself . . .'

She walked over to Mademoiselle Rose. 'Tell me something.'

'Yes?'

'That boy, my cousin . . . and her . . . I've guessed right, haven't I?'

Mademoiselle Rose flinched and pursed her pale little lips in a violent attempt at denial. 'No, no, Hélène,' she murmured feebly.

But Hélène whispered passionately in her ear, 'I know, I know, I'm telling you I know.'

A door opened behind them. Mademoiselle Rose shuddered and fearfully squeezed her hand. 'Be quiet,' she said softly, 'be quiet now. If they ever realised you suspected you'd be sent away to boarding school, my poor darling, and as for me . . .'

Hélène lowered her eyes, frozen with fear. 'Don't be silly . . .'

But she was thinking, 'I'd be happier at boarding school. There's nowhere I could be more miserable than in this house! But Mademoiselle Rose, my poor Mademoiselle Rose, what would she do without me? I'm not the one who needs her any more,' she thought suddenly with cold, bleak lucidity. 'I don't need to be tucked into bed, looked after, hugged . . . I've grown up, got older . . . How old you can feel at twelve . . .'

She felt a sudden yearning for solitude, for silence, for an intense melancholy that would fill her soul until it overflowed with sadness and hatred.

'If it weren't for Mademoiselle Rose, no one could hurt me. She's the only thing they can use against me. But I'm all she has. I think she would die without me.'

She clenched her fists; she felt small and weak, emotionally vulnerable, and this feeling of powerlessness filled her with rebellion and despair.

She went into the schoolroom next door; it contained cupboards, built for her mother's clothes; a slight odour of camphor came from the wardrobe where she kept her furs. Everywhere Hélène went she found her mother.

She slammed the door shut, went back into her room, walked over to the window and looked out with a kind of gloomy horror at the torrents of rain pouring out of the dark sky; tears streamed down her cheeks.

'You know that she . . . Mama has always said how happy she is to have you . . .' she finally said, her voice shaking.

'I know that,' murmured Mademoiselle Rose, 'but . . .'

She was standing in the middle of the room, small and frail in her black dress. She studied Hélène's face with sad tenderness, but gradually her eyes became glassy and vacant. She seemed to be looking for something very far away, beyond

Hélène's face, visions that only she could see. A past long gone . . . or the frightening future in this cold, inhospitable place: solitude, exile, old age. She sighed and whispered absent-mindedly, 'Come along now, hang up your coat. Don't throw your hat on the bed. Come here so I can tidy your hair . . .'

As always, she took solace in the most humble, everyday tasks, but she seemed to be doing them with a kind of anxiety and nervous determination that surprised Hélène. She unpacked the bags, folded the gloves and stockings and put them into a drawer, refusing to allow the servants to help her.

'Tell them to leave me in peace, Hélène.'

'She's changed since the war started,' thought Hélène.

# 2

1914 and 1915 came and went at a slow and deadly pace . . .

One evening Max came into the dining room where Hélène was sitting in a large armchair, half buried in newspapers. Wartime newspapers had entire columns left blank; no one else in the house looked at them, except for Karol who read the Stock Market listings on the last page. Max smiled. She was a funny little thing . . . She had a small, flat chest, slim, gangly arms poking through the short sleeves of her blue wool dress; a German-style white cambric smock with large deep pleats covered her body; her black hair was set in thick curls round her face, which was beginning to take on the cadaverous complexion of all St Petersburg children who were brought up without air, light or any form of exercise other than an hour's ice skating on Sundays.

When she noticed him, she quickly took off a pair of glasses that made her look even older and uglier: her eyes were weak, worn out by the bright electric lights that were kept on from dawn.

He burst out laughing. 'You wear glasses? How funny you look, my poor little thing. You look like a little old lady.'

'I only wear them when I'm working or reading,' she said, feeling a rush of blood to her cheeks.

He took cruel, mocking pleasure in her embarrassment: 'You do care about the way you look! Poor little thing,' he said again and the scornful sympathy in his voice sent a shudder of anger through Hélène's soul.

'Where's your mother?'

She pointed sullenly to the next room, but at that very moment the door opened and Bella came in, wearing a lace dressing gown that barely concealed her breasts; she stretched out her hand for Max to kiss. As they stared at each other in silence, Max slowly half closed his eyes and parted his lips with a look of intense desire.

'And they imagine I see nothing? Unbelievable,' thought Hélène.

They went into the sitting room; Hélène sat down again in the red armchair and continued reading the papers. Was there anyone here, other than she and Mademoiselle Rose, who remembered there was a war on? Money kept pouring in; wine was overflowing. Who gave a thought to the wounded men, the women in mourning? Who heard the footsteps of troops in the street as dawn broke, the sad sound of soldiers marching towards death?

She looked at the time. Eight-thirty. Lessons and home-work had filled the entire day since morning, without a moment's rest. But she loved studying and books, the way other people love wine for its power to make you forget. What else did she have? She lived in a deserted, silent house. The sound of her own footsteps in the empty rooms, the silence of the cold streets beyond the closed windows, the rain and the snow, the early darkness, the green lamp beside her that burned throughout the long evenings and which she watched for hours on end until its light began to waver before her weary eyes: this was the setting for her life. Her father was almost never there; her mother came home in the evening and locked herself away in the sitting room with Max; Bella had no women friends: in wartime, people had other things to worry about than the happiness of children . . .

A servant came in to close the curtains; in the next room she could hear Max's muffled laughter.

'What are the two of them doing in there?' she thought. 'But what does it matter, as long as they leave me the hell alone . . .'

She could smell cigarette smoke from under the door; her father wasn't home yet; he'd get back between nine and ten o'clock and they'd eat meals that were either cold or burned; he would bring home men whom Hélène knew under the generic term of 'business associates', nervous, anxious men with impatient eyes and hands as taut and grasping as claws; she closed her eyes, imagining she could already hear the word they endlessly spoke, the only word Hélène understood, the word she heard again and again, buzzing around her, the word that invaded her waking moments and her dreams: 'Millions . . . millions . . . millions . . .'

The servant stopped at the entrance to the room, looked at the clock and shook her head. 'Does Mademoiselle know what time her father will be getting home?'

'No, I don't,' said Hélène.

She pulled back the curtain and looked out into the street, trying to catch a glimpse of the carriage lights in the snow.

Little by little, everything around her faded away. She sank into a delicious trance, as she had done in the past when she'd played at being Napoleon. But now, other dreams filled her mind, dreams that returned again and again, imperious dreams of domination: to be a queen, to be a feared statesman, to be the most beautiful woman in the world . . . This last dream was new; she approached it with caution, as if it contained some mysterious fire.

'Will I be beautiful? No, certainly not,' she mused sadly. 'I'm at that unattractive age now, when it's impossible to be pretty. But I'll never be beautiful; my mouth's too big and I have an ugly complexion. Dear Lord, please make every man fall in love with me when I grow up . . .'

She shuddered: her father had just come in, followed by two men, Slivker, a Jew with jet-black eyes whose arm shook when he talked, as if he were still carrying the bundle of rugs he undoubtedly used to hawk on café terraces; the other man was Alexander Pavlovitch Chestov, the son of one of the short-lived Ministers of War of the period.

Hélène sat down at her place, next to Mademoiselle Rose. The dining table was weighed down by heavy silver place settings, bought at auction, for the old aristocracy had managed to lose all its money and was selling just about everything it owned to the newly wealthy businessmen.

'Everything in this house is second-hand, like in a thieves' den,' mused Hélène; the heavy silver pieces came from various sales; they hadn't bothered to remove the initials, coronets or family crests that decorated them; only their weight interested the Karols. Capo di Monte porcelain groups sat in a corner, still in their wrapping paper; the sideboard was piled with Sèvres statuettes and delicate pink plates decorated with figures and flowers; Bella had bought them the week before at auction, but they just sat there sadly, unused, wrapped in straw and tissue paper. All the books in the library had been bought by the yard and no one except Hélène opened the leather-bound volumes emblazoned with gilt tooling.

'Where could we buy some portraits of ancestors?' joked Bella.

Only the furs brought back from Siberia were new. Each ermine pelt that now adorned her mother's coat had once been a scrap of fur, the remains of a dead animal, which Hélène had seen emptied on to the table and rummaged through by greedy hands.

'Alexander Pavlovitch . . .'

'Salomon Arkadievitch . . .'

Chestov's eyes were full of disdain when he spoke; he seemed afraid to raise his long head with its fine blond hair covered in pomade, as if the company of these Jews poisoned the air; Slivker returned his scornful look, though tempered by fear.

Adding to the clutter of the dining room were the bouquets and arrangements of flowers sent to Karol's wife; because he had become so rich since the beginning of the war, everyone pandered to him.

On her way to her place at the table, Bella picked up a red rose and placed it in Max's buttonhole. Her lace dress gaped open slightly, revealing her bosom; she slowly pulled it closed: her breasts were beautiful.

The butler came in, followed by an underling who carried the soup in a silver tureen that bore the Besborodko family coat of arms; the glasses were Baccarat, but all of them were chipped; no one took any notice; everyone seemed to sense that such wealth was fleeting: since it had come out of nowhere, it could just as easily disappear in a cloud of smoke.

Mademoiselle Rose leaned in towards Hélène. 'Have you read the papers?' she whispered anxiously.

'Yes. It's always the same thing,' Hélène said sadly. 'They're "treading water" . . .'

'You don't understand,' Slivker was saying. 'For us, the war is a bit of good luck. Those bits of paper you play around with will be worth less than that tomorrow,' he said, pointing to the vase of fragrant, dark-red roses that decorated the table. 'What the war needs, what's important to war, are arms, munitions, weapons, cannons. And besides, it's our patriotic duty!'

'And what if the war ends in a month?' Chestov bellowed shrilly. 'We'd be left with all that stock on our hands . . .'

'If we always worried about tomorrow . . .' said Slivker, laughing, pushing away his empty plate.

The Minister's son took his monocle out of his pocket; he turned it over in his hands, slowly, affectionately, as if it were a flower, before placing it over his eye and fixing it there with a sudden contraction of his facial muscles. Throwing Slivker a look of aristocratic scorn, he leaned towards Bella. 'Our conversation isn't very interesting for Madame,' he said amiably, in French.

'She's used to it,' said Slivker.

'It isn't wise to have dealings in the things you were talking about,' Karol interjected. 'That's up to the department of National Defence. No, what's important are uniforms for the soldiers, boots, food . . .'

The butler brought in the sturgeon in aspic, arranged on a bed of herbs and garnished with golden egg yolks, accompanied by a silver sauceboat decorated in bas-relief with little shepherds and bagpipes.

They ate for a while in silence. Hélène looked up and heard Slivker say, '. . . Some business about cannons . . . In Spain, they have some cannons that date back to 1860, but they're still in excellent condition, it must be said. Apparently, they can aim better than the ones we have now.' He'd wolfed down the fish in two bites, then grabbed one of the two glasses of wine set before him without caring which one it was. It was a sweet Barsac that the Karols always served with fish; he gulped it down, then grimaced in disgust; he was teetotal, didn't smoke and would never had gone near a woman, or played cards, or eaten pork if circumstances hadn't forced him to seek out the company of members of the government. Government officials, it seemed, could only understand business matters when surrounded by food or women.

'Live with the dogs, not like them,' he sometimes told Karol, since Karol loved gambling, wine and women. 'They'll be the death of you.'

'Brilliant deal, big money . . . Could tell you about it, if you're interested . . .' he continued. 'Wonderful cannons,' he said, finally allowing himself to get carried away, as was his nature, and singing the praises of the strange cannons as if he were selling stockings outside the entrance to some building.

'But, for goodness sake, they were made in 1860!'

'Why do you think they would be worse than the ones we have now? Don't you think that our fathers were as sly as you and me? Why wouldn't they have been? Where's your evidence?'

'If I might say something,' said Chestov, carefully choosing a glass of wine and drinking it slowly, a smile on his pursed lips and a look of scorn in his eyes. 'You . . .'

'No, *you* allow *me* to say something. We must keep everybody's role straight. After all, it's not up to me to say whether these cannons are good or bad. *I'm* not an engineer. *I'm* not an artilleryman. I'm a "speculator", a businessman. That's my part in all this,' he said, turning his back on Chestov to help himself to the partridge in cream sauce that was being offered to him; he smelled the salad and sent it away with a gesture of disgust, for he didn't like the look of it.

'I go to the War Ministry,' he continued. 'I say, "Here's the situation. I've been offered this or that. Are you interested? Look into it and see if it's suitable." I wouldn't take on such responsibility myself, what an idea. You want it? This is how much it costs. You don't want it? Good evening, then. Naturally, it is essential that they understand . . . that *everyone*,' he said, emphasising the word while staring fixedly and ironically at Chestov, 'that *everyone* understands what is in his own best interest.'

'What is in the interest of Russia,' Chestov said harshly and looked around him, haughtily scrutinising everyone as if to remind them all that he was the representative of the government and had the right to look deep into their hearts and souls in the name of the Emperor.

'Naturally,' they all said at once. 'Speaking of which, has anyone read the papers?'

'Bring them here,' Bella said to one of the servants.

They passed them round, each of them skimming the

headlines before carefully looking at the Stock Market page, then impatiently crumpled them up and threw them on the floor where the young servant collected them with a silver-gilt dustpan and brush that bore the coat of arms of Count Petschersky.

'Nothing new,' said Max. 'It's the next Hundred Years' War.' He looked at Bella with sensuous desire. 'How wonderful these roses smell . . .'

'They're the ones you sent,' Bella said. She smiled and pointed to the delicate silver filigree basket where the roses were opening their petals in the warmth around the table.

Meanwhile, Chestov was saying, 'As far as the cannons are concerned, I do not share your enthusiasm, my dear . . . er . . .' He hesitated, pretended to be trying to remember a name he'd forgotten. '. . . er . . . Salomon Salomonovitch . . .'

Slivker understood the insinuation but merely shrugged his shoulders as if he were thinking, 'You can call me a pig if you like, just do as you're told.'

'Arkadievitch, dear sir, Arkadievitch,' he said affably, correcting the Minister's son, 'but never mind. You were saying?'

'Your cannons, perhaps they might serve some other purpose? It seems to me they could be stripped down and used as scrap metal. I'm only a layman in such matters, of course, but I do believe we are short of scrap iron.'

Slivker, having achieved his aim, allowed himself to pause for breath; he took his time choosing some asparagus and waited quite a while before replying. 'Would you care to speak to your father about it? My God, it wouldn't commit you to anything . . . Of course he wouldn't buy anything without thinking it over first . . .'

'But he's not the only one at the Ministry . . .'

'Oh! You know, it's only a matter of persuading the others.'

'You mean bribing them,' said Karol; he called a spade a spade.

'Alas!'

'The country's in such a sad state,' said Slivker who was only too happy to flatter Chestov now that he had got what he wanted.

'When it's an important matter of patriotism, as in this case, it's not such a bad thing, but if you only knew . . . However, I can't betray the secrets of the gods,' said Chestov.

'I know about a deal that's better than your Spanish cannons. It's a factory that was confiscated from an Austrian group at the beginning of the war and which is going to start operating again. I have it from a reliable source; they're selling all the shares as one lot; they'll cost 5 but will be worth 500 in two months,' said Karol. 'I don't understand why people aren't willing to get involved in sound business deals.'

'Because', Slivker said bitterly, 'when you first get involved in a deal, you never know if it will turn out well.'

'For example,' said Karol, smiling sarcastically, 'your bread deal with the army.'

'What about it?'

'You made us listen to you go on about it for six months. It ended up as a heap of rotten bread.'

'The flour was of the finest quality,' said Slivker, who seemed annoyed. 'I used only the best millers. What went wrong was that they decided to save money on building the ovens, and since no one knew the exact dimensions to build them, the bread wasn't cooked properly and went off.'

'And soldiers died of dysentery,' said Chestov.

'Is that what you think? Well, the merchandise was rejected and that was the end of it; it was unfortunate, but the bread had to be thrown away. I insisted upon it myself to the authorities. I don't have the death of a single man on *my* conscience,' said Slivker.

Karol laughed like a child, his face contorting in a malicious grimace; he reached over the table and gave a little tug at Hélène's hair; she grabbed the tanned, dry hand as he was pulling it away and kissed it. She loved the fire in his eyes, his white hair and his smile: it could be so sad and so mischievous.

'Although, whenever he looks at that woman, he melts,' Hélène thought resentfully. 'Is it possible he doesn't see through their charade? He's actually happy, happy in this chaotic household, among the new furniture, the dining service engraved with initials that aren't his, betrayed by an unfaithful wife . . . You can't say he doesn't see it . . . No, it's not that; he just brushes it aside, ignores it . . . In the end, there's only one thing in the world he's passionate about and it's slowly eating away at his soul: gambling, whether on the Stock Market or cards. And that's all there is to it.'

They ate the apple charlotte, which was covered in hot chocolate sauce. Hélène loved chocolate and for a moment she stopped 'listening to the conversation of adults' as her mother put it when reproaching her.

'Max also says that you're too interested in hearing about business deals,' her mother sometimes said. 'Are they any of your concern? Think about your lessons instead.'

Hélène, out of pure perversity, put her heart and soul into listening and understanding what she heard.

But she was tired; all she could make out was some vague mumbling.

'Ships . . .'

'Petrol . . .'

'Pipelines . . .'

'Boots . . .'

'Sleeping bags . . .'

'Shares . . .'

'. . . Millions . . . Millions . . . Millions . . .'

This last word constantly returned, punctuating their sentences like the chorus of a song. 'An old song,' Hélène thought wearily.

Dinner was over; Hélène left the table, gave a shy little curtsey that no one noticed and went to bed. The smell of cigars and brandy wafted through the house until morning, slipping beneath her door and insinuating itself into her dreams. A faraway rumbling shook the paving stones: artillery detachments were passing by in the street.

# 3

The revolution hadn't yet begun, but everyone could sense it was imminent; even the air they breathed seemed heavy and full of a kind of menace, as dawn is on the day of a storm. No one was interested in news from the Front; the war seemed to have retreated into the distant past; the wounded were looked on with indifference, the soldiers with sullen hostility. Hélène came into contact with men who were passionate only about money. They were all getting rich. Money flowed like the Pactolus River, with such an impetuous, stormy, capricious force that it terrified everyone who lived along its banks who quenched their thirst with its waters. It flowed too quickly, too easily . . . The moment you bought some shares on the Stock Market they shot up like a fever. People no longer took pleasure in shouting out the figures in front of Hélène: they whispered them instead. She no longer heard 'millions', but 'billions', spoken in low voices that were hesitant, breathless; all around her she saw only expressions of greed and fear.

They bought everything at once. Anything, anywhere.

Noon until night, men would arrive, pulling packages from their pockets; behind closed doors, Hélène could hear muffled voices involved in rushed, intense discussions about numbers. They bought fur pelts that hadn't even been cleaned or sewn, just tied together with string and hung on a long rod, the way salesmen from Asia had sold them in some faraway bazaar; they bought ermine and sable pelts, chinchilla in lots that looked like rat skins, gemstones, necklaces, antique bracelets, all valued according to their weight, enormous emeralds, but cloudy, since their greed and haste were stronger than their judgement; they bought gold: in bars, in ingots, but most especially they bought shares, piles and piles of them, representing holdings in banks, tankers, pipelines and in diamonds that still lay buried beneath the ground. Pieces of paper poked out of the furniture. They made the walls and beds bulge; they were hidden in the servants' rooms, in the study, at the backs of cupboards and, when spring came, in wood-burning stoves; wads of shares were sewn into the fabric of armchairs and the men who came to the Karols' house took turns sitting on them, warming them with the heat of their bodies as if they were trying to hatch golden eggs. In the corner of the sitting room great bundles of paper were rolled up in the Savonnerie carpet decorated with garlands of roses; they rustled whenever there was a draft. Hélène sometimes amused herself by stepping on them to make them crunch, the way you crush dead leaves beneath your shoes in autumn. The white piano, its cover closed, shimmered faintly in the shadows; on the walls were motifs in gold: reed-pipes, bagpipes, hats in the style of Louis XV, shepherd's crooks, ribbons, bouquets of flowers, all gathering dust. Hélène's parents, the 'businessmen' and Max spent every evening in the stuffy little room that Karol used as an office. It contained nothing but a telephone and a typewriter. They piled in there, happy to breathe in the thick cigar smoke, happy to hear the bare floorboards creak beneath their feet, happy to look at the plain walls that were thick enough to muffle their discussions.

Sitting side by side in that narrow room, Max and Bella took advantage of the chaos and the dim light, which came from a single light bulb hanging down on a wire, to press their warm thighs, their warm bodies against each other. Karol noticed nothing, but every now and again he would squeeze his wife's bare arm affectionately in the dim light; she respected him now, and feared him, for he was the source of luxury and comfort. Yet she didn't feel any more at ease in this house than Hélène; sometimes she was overcome with nostalgia for a hotel room, two packing cases piled in a corner and brief affairs embarked on by chance. Her Max was so impatient, so young; his beautiful body never grew tired; she encouraged his jealousy, his rage, his passion for her. Hélène found herself back among the arguments and quarrels that had been her lullabies as a very young child, but now they were between her mother and Max, and were imbued with a bitter intensity that annoyed her and which she couldn't understand. Nevertheless, she forced herself to irritate them as much as possible; she had a derisive way of looking at Max that infuriated him; she never spoke to him; he started to hate her; he was only twenty-four and still childish enough to hate a little girl.

Hélène wandered sadly through all the rooms, waiting for dinner time. She had finished all her lessons; Mademoiselle Rose took the book from her hands. 'You'll ruin your eyes, Lili . . .'

It was true that, now and again, reading affected her too much, as if she were heavily intoxicated. But to sit in the schoolroom and do nothing, while Mademoiselle Rose sat in silence opposite her, gently nodding her head without saying a word, was beyond her. For a while she sat patiently, watching Mademoiselle's skilful, ageing hands, which were always busy with some sewing; then, little by little, a desperate desire to do something, to have a change of scene, made her rush out of the room. Mademoiselle Rose had aged so much since the war. She hadn't had any news of her family for three years and her brother, the one she called 'little Marcel', for he was her half-brother after her father's second marriage, had disappeared in the Vosges region of France at the beginning of 1914. She had no friends in St Petersburg; she didn't even understand the language of the country despite having lived there for nearly fifteen years. Everything upset her. Her entire life was dedicated to Hélène's well-being, but Hélène was growing up. She needed to be cared for in other ways, but Mademoiselle Rose had known her since she was so very young, and was herself so innately reserved and with such a strong sense of propriety that she was unable to reach out to Hélène, to encourage confidences which, at that point in her life, Hélène wouldn't have entrusted to her anyway.

Hélène protected her inner life; she hid it fiercely from sight – everyone's sight, even from the person she loved most in the world. She and Mademoiselle Rose were bound together by a fear that neither of them dared to speak of: that Mademoiselle Rose might be sent away. Anything was possible. Their lives were ruled by Bella's whims, by her excessively bad moods or a sarcastic remark from Max.

During these deadly years Hélène did not once breathe freely; there wasn't a single night when she went to bed feeling calm and confident. During the day, Mademoiselle Rose took Hélène to mass at the church of Notre-Dame-de-France. A French priest spoke to a small congregation of people born in this foreign land; he spoke of France, of the war, and prayed for 'those who suffer, those who must travel, and the soldiers who have fallen on the battlefields'.

'We're fine,' thought Hélène in between responses; she looked at the two low candles burning beneath the image of the Virgin Mary, and listened to the soft crackling of the wax tears that flowed and flowed, ever so slowly, until they fell on to the paving stones. She closed her eyes. At home, Bella would say, shrugging her shoulders, 'Your Mademoiselle Rose is becoming holier-than-thou. That's all we need . . .'

In church Hélène feared nothing, thought about nothing, allowed herself to be cradled by a soothing dream, but the moment she stepped outside and found herself in the dark street, walking along the gloomy, fetid canal, her heart ached with mortal anguish once more.

Sometimes Mademoiselle Rose looked around in surprise, as if she were waking from a dream. Sometimes she would murmur a few vague words, and when Hélène impatiently cried, 'What do you mean?' she would shudder and turn her large, deep-set eyes slowly away. 'Nothing, Hélène, nothing,' she would say softly.

Yet the pity that filled Hélène's heart did not soften it; she bore the pity angrily, as if it were a burden. 'I'm becoming horrible, now,' she thought in despair, 'just like everyone else.'

In the mirrors of the sitting room, lit up by the light that filtered in from beneath the office next door, Hélène studied her reflection for a long time: her face and the dark-coloured dress that looked like a black stain against the delicate light wood panelling, her thin, tanned neck that stuck out of the narrow collar of her checked dress, the gold chain and blue enamel locket that, to Hélène, were the only 'outward signs' of wealth. She was so bored. She believed she was unhappy because they dressed her like a little girl in short skirts, with her hair in great curls, although in Russia, a girl was already considered a woman at fourteen. As for the rest . . .

'What am I complaining about?' she thought. 'I'm no different from anyone else. Of course, everyone's house has an adulterous wife, unhappy children and busy men who think only of money. With money, everyone flatters you, smiles at you, everything works out, that's what they all say. I have money, I'm healthy, but I'm bored.'

One evening Chestov found her in this state of mind and walked over to her; he was drunk; he looked at her slim face raised towards him and smiled. 'Such beautiful eyes,' he said.

Hélène knew he was drunk and worse, that he was despicable, selling his country to the highest bidder. But he was the first man who had noticed her. She couldn't explain how she felt. It was the first time she could feel the impact of a man's eyes on her, the way he looked at her face, then down at her chest where his gaze lingered on her budding breasts, straining beneath her dress. For a long time Chestov's gaze sought the tender spot between her chest and her shoulder, still small and angular like a young girl's; he took her hand and kissed it, then left. That night, for the first time in her life, Hélène wasn't able to sleep, feeling ashamed, unhappy, troubled to the point of suffering, and yet so proud, still feeling, there in the darkness, the heavy, insolent gaze of a man upon her. Yet from that moment on, Chestov made her feel more and more afraid and she did everything she could to avoid him.

On another evening she saw groups of women marching through the city asking for bread. They walked behind a scrap of material that billowed in the wind and the sound that rose from the crowd was not a clamour but rather a muffled, timid pleading: 'Bread, bread, we want bread . . .'

As they passed, all the doors closed one by one.

Hélène could hear them in the room next door saying, '. . . Buy . . . sell . . .' 'I've heard . . .' 'They say that . . .' 'Unrest, riots, a revolution . . .'

But deep inside they didn't believe it; they were as irrational as men being swept along by a flood.

'We'll always have money . . .'

'There's only one thing to do . . . buy, buy . . .'

'Buy anything . . . electric light bulbs, toothbrushes, jars of jam . . . I was recently told about a Rembrandt. They'd sell it for a piece of bread . . .'

Riots? They brushed the idea aside with a wave of the hand; they didn't ignore it; they didn't underestimate it, but that impatient wave of the hand meant 'Yes, yes. But we know very well that it can't last. Yes, yes. We can tell, just as you can, that it will all end, fade away. In any case we're used to it. Stability is rather boring, frightens us. We understand, we understand perfectly well, but what prods us along, what we enjoy, is to gamble on the future, on the symbols of wealth, on the diamonds that will be confiscated, with stocks and shares that soon might only be worth the paper they're printed on, on paintings that might be burned . . .'

'I've heard that Rasputin has been murdered,' someone said quietly. 'They say he was assassinated by . . .'

Then there was a vague whispering: to them, a halo of respect and terror still surrounded the Emperor and the Imperial family.

'Is it possible?'

A moment of shock, then they brushed it aside. 'Yes, yes, we'll have to see. For the moment, let us get on with gambling, getting intoxicated, piling up our gold, our jewellery, or at least let us talk about money, dream about money, amorously stroke our gold bars, our gemstones, our roubles . . . What will they be worth tomorrow? What will they be worth? Ah, tomorrow is tomorrow . . . What's the point of thinking of tomorrow? We have to sell, sell, sell . . . We have to buy, buy, buy . . .'

'Dear Lord, please protect Papa . . .'

Her mother was never included.

'Dear Lord, please protect Mademoiselle Rose . . . Forgive me for my sins. Please let the French win the war . . .'

# 4

The February Revolution came and went, then the October Revolution. The city was distraught, buried in snow. It was a Sunday in autumn. Lunch was over. Max was there. Thick cigar smoke filled the room. You could hear the gentle crackling of the wads of American dollars and British pounds sewn into the armchairs. It was three o'clock; they were drinking very expensive cognac in brandy glasses. Everyone was silent, half listening to the dull, distant gunfire that echoed from the suburbs, day and night, though no one paid any attention to it any more.

Karol had pulled Hélène on to his knee. She had been there for a while, and he had forgotten she was there; he stroked her absent-mindedly, the way you play with a dog's ears. And sometimes, while he was talking, he pulled her hair so hard that Hélène trembled in pain; he was rough in his affection, but Hélène bore it without complaining, happy to be able to irritate her mother. Nevertheless, she wanted to get down from his lap; he held her back.

'Wait a while. You never sit with me.'

'I have lessons to prepare, Papa,' she said, kissing his tanned hand and its long, slender fingers; he wore an old-fashioned, wide, round wedding ring, the symbol of slavery.

'Learn your lessons here then.'

'All right, Papa.'

He slipped a small sugar cube dipped in cognac into her mouth. 'This is for you, Hélène.' Then immediately forgot about her again.

They talked about Shanghai, Tehran, Constantinople. They had to leave. But where should they go? Danger was everywhere, but since everyone was in the same boat it seemed less urgent; it would pass. Hélène wasn't listening; she was completely indifferent to the name of some distant corner of the world where she would end up. She had got down from his lap and was sitting in the red armchair now, learning her lesson for the next day. It was from a book on 'German Conversation' and she had to memorise '*die zwanzigste Lektion*', the description of a close-knit family. Hélène repeated the words quietly: '*Eine glückliche Familie* (a happy family). *Der Vater* (the father) *ist ein frommer Mann* (is a pious man) . . .

'Good Lord!' she thought. 'What imbeciles . . .'

She looked at the illustration that accompanied the text.

The 'happy family' all sat together in a blue sitting room; the father, who had a blond curly beard that came down to his chest, wore a frock coat and slippers, and was reading the newspapers beside the fireplace; the mother, the *Hausfrau*, was dusting the bookcase shelves, wearing a long apron tied at the waist; the young girl was playing the piano while the schoolboy learned his lessons by the light of a lamp; two young children, a yellow dog and a grey cat sat on the rug in the middle of the room, all 'playing', according to the text, 'the innocent games appropriate to their age'.

'What a fantasy!' thought Hélène.

She looked at the people around her. They didn't even see she was there, but to her as well they were unreal, distant, half-hidden in a mist: vain, insubstantial ghosts lacking flesh and blood; she lived on the sidelines, far away from them, in an imaginary world where she was mistress and queen. She picked up the small pencil that she always kept in her pocket, hesitated, then gradually, very gradually, pulled the book close to her, as if it were a loaded weapon.

She started to write:

> The father is thinking about a woman he met in the street, and the mother has only just said goodbye to her lover. They do not understand their children, and their children do not love them; the young girl is thinking about the boy she's in love with, and the boy about the naughty words he has learned at school. The little children will grow up and be just like them. Books lie. There is no virtue, no love in the world. Every household is the same. In every family there is nothing but greed, lies and mutual misunderstanding.

She stopped, twiddled the pencil round in her hand and a cruel, shy smile spread across her face. It made her feel better to write these things down. No one paid any attention to her or cared about her. She could amuse herself in any way she pleased; she continued writing, barely pressing down on the pencil, but with a strange rapidity and dexterity she had never experienced before, an agility of thought that made her aware of what she was writing and what was taking shape in her mind simultaneously, so they suddenly coincided. She experimented with this new game, as if she were watching tears flow down her face on to her hands on a winter's evening and seeing how the frost transformed them into icy flowers.

It's the same everywhere. In our house as well, it's the same. The husband, the wife and . . .

She hesitated, then wrote: 'The lover . . .'

She rubbed out the last word, then wrote it in again, enthralled as it appeared before her eyes, then disguised it once more by adding little arrows and curlicues to each letter until the word disappeared and looked like a small insect with a mass of antennae, or a plant with many thorns. It had an evil air about it, strange, secretive and crude, that pleased her.

'What are you writing, Hélène?'

She gave an involuntary start, and they all stared at her with surprise and suspicion as her face slowly turned white, looking old before its time and suddenly exhausted.

'Now, then . . . What are you writing? Give it to me,' Bella commanded.

Hélène clenched her hands together and silently began twisting and tearing up the paper.

Bella pounced. 'I said give it to me!'

Desperately, Hélène tried to crumple the paper between her trembling fingers but it was too thick; the coloured illustration on the glossy paper creased but wouldn't tear; terrified, she breathed in the smell of glue and heavy coloured ink that she would never forget . . .

'You're mad! You will give that to me at once! Be careful, Hélène!' shouted Bella in a rage and, grabbing her daughter's shoulder, she dug her nails into her with such fury that Hélène could feel their sharp tips pierce her flesh through her dress. But she clung on to the book, without shedding a tear, teeth clenched, until suddenly she dropped it and it fell to the floor.

Bella made a dive for the page Hélène had torn out, read the few sentences written in pencil, and looked in astonishment at the illustration. Blood rushed straight to her pale face, visible despite her thick make-up. 'She's gone mad,' she exclaimed. 'You miserable thing, you ungrateful little hussy. You're a horrible liar! You're nothing but a fool, do you hear me? Nothing but a wretched idiot. When someone thinks, dares to think such things, things that are so impertinent, so stupid, they at least shouldn't write them down. They keep them to themselves. How dare you judge your parents. And we're such good parents. We sacrifice everything for you, for your sake. We worry ourselves sick over your health, your happiness. How ungrateful of you! Do you even understand what it is like to be a parent? You should cherish us! You should think there is nothing dearer to you in the world!'

'To top it all off,' Hélène thought bitterly, 'they want to be loved.'

Her mother's face was convulsed with fury; she leaned in towards Hélène, her hated eyes burning, dilated with anger and fear. 'Is there anything you don't have, you ungrateful thing? Look at you! You have books, dresses, jewellery. What about this?' she shouted, tearing the little blue enamel locket from its chain and sending it rolling on to the floor; she crushed it with her heel, stamped on it in a rage.

'Look at her, look at that face! Not a word of regret! Not a single tear! Just you wait. *I* know how to bring you to heel. All this is your governess's fault. She's turning you against your parents. She's teaching you to hate us. Well, she can just pack her bags, do you hear me? You can say goodbye to your Mademoiselle Rose. You'll never see her again! Ah, so that makes you cry, does it? Look at her, Boris! Look at your wonderful daughter. Not a tear for me, for her mother, or for you. But as soon as it concerns Mademoiselle Rose she's all contrite. Ah, so you deign to speak now. And what have you got to say for yourself, let's hear it!'

'It wasn't her, Mama! Mama, it's all my fault!'

'Shut up!'

'Forgive me, Mama,' cried Hélène; she sensed that only her humbleness was a precious enough offering to appease the wrath of the gods.

'They can do whatever they want to me,' she thought in despair. 'She can beat me, she can kill me, but not that.'

'Mama, please forgive me, it will never happen again,' she cried, finding the words she found hardest to say because of her pride, the words of a chastised child. 'I'm begging you to forgive me.'

But when she saw Hélène's resistance collapse, Bella allowed herself to fly into a rage. Or perhaps she thought her tears and shouting would stun her husband, divert his attention from Max?

She ran to the door, opened it and shouted, 'Mademoiselle! Come here at once!'

Mademoiselle Rose ran in; she was shaking. She hadn't heard anything; she looked at Hélène in terror and asked what was wrong.

'What's wrong?' cried Bella. 'What's wrong is that this child . . . this child is an ungrateful liar. And you're the one who has brought the creature up. I congratulate you. But I've had enough, enough of this. I've put up with everything, but this is the final straw. You will leave, do you hear me! I'll show you that I am the mistress in this house!'

Mademoiselle Rose listened to her without saying a word. She didn't even turn white: it was impossible for her pallid face to get any paler. She still appeared to be listening even after Bella had stopped talking. The furious words seemed to awaken an echo that only she could hear. 'Very well, Madam,' she said quietly, sounding weary.

Max, who hadn't said a word until then, shrugged his shoulders. 'Oh, let them be, Bella. You're making a mountain out of a molehill.'

'Get out!' Bella shouted at her daughter, and she slapped her silent, motionless face, her nails leaving red marks. Hélène let out a yelp, but she refused to cry; she turned towards her father. He was still holding the book covered in writing. He said nothing. He was standing up, and what broke Hélène's heart, filled it with remorse, was the movement backwards he made, crushing himself against the wall, as if he wanted to disappear, to fade away into the darkness.

Hélène walked over to him and quietly whispered, 'Papa, do you want me to tell you what the word was, the word you couldn't see?'

He pushed her away angrily and spoke as quietly as she had: 'No.'

Then, softly, his mouth clenched shut like hers (by which she understood that he didn't want to know anything, that he preferred to continue loving this woman and this caricature of a home, preferred to keep the only illusion he had left on this earth), he said, 'Go away! You're a very bad girl.'

# 5

As she did every evening, Mademoiselle Rose stood at Hélène's bedside and picked up the candle. As she did every evening, she said calmly, 'Go to sleep quickly now and try not to think about anything.'

She gently stroked Hélène's forehead with her warm hand, as she'd done for the past eleven years, using the same instinctive gesture; then she sighed and got into her own bed.

Hélène's heart was breaking. For a long time she looked in despair at Mademoiselle Rose's calm face in the candlelight; yet she wasn't asleep. Like Hélène, she was undoubtedly listening to the clock chime the hours; she was breathing in the smell of smoke that filtered into the room from under the door; in the next room Hélène's parents were talking quietly. From her bed, the little girl could hear an occasional outburst.

'It isn't true, Boris, I swear to you, it isn't true.'

She was such a good liar . . .

'You can see how ungrateful children are,' Hélène heard her continue. 'She cares more about a foreigner, a scheming woman, than she does about us. It's that Frenchwoman who's driving her away from us.'

Then she could only make out some vague whispering, the sound of crying, the weary voice of her father. 'Calm down now, Bella, my darling . . .'

'I swear to you that he's just a child, a child who loves me. Is that my fault? You know me, come on . . . I like being attractive, it's true, but as far as I'm concerned, he's just a child. You can understand that it sometimes amuses me to tease him, but you'd have to have the dirty mind of a young girl or an old woman to think . . . I love you, Boris. You do believe me, don't you?'

Hélène heard Karol sigh deeply. 'Of course I do, of course . . .'

'Then kiss me, don't look at me like that.'

The sound of kisses. The candle went out.

'She'll die,' Hélène thought in despair. 'She can't live without me. She's alone, all alone. How can they not understand what they're doing? How can they not see that they're killing a human being? Oh, I hate them,' she said, meaning her mother and Max. 'How I hate them . . .' She wrung her weak, trembling hands. 'I'd like to kill them,' she murmured.

Outside, a group of anarchist terrorists in an old Ford decorated with a skeleton's head drove past her room, making the little white bookcase and the silly statuettes that decorated it shake. They fired a machine gun into the empty streets. But no one was listening to them. Behind closed windows exhausted men, reluctantly resigned to everything, were sleeping.

All next day Bella refused to say a word in Hélène's presence. Karol wasn't at home. An innate sense of propriety prevented Hélène from saying a word about Mademoiselle Rose. Another day passed. Mademoiselle Rose was packing her trunks. Yet life carried on so normally, just as in certain delirious dreams when terror merges with familiar details. Hélène learned her lessons; she sat opposite her mother for meals; the electricity had been cut off for weeks; the dim flame of a candle flickered at the back of the enormous dark room. Between noon and two o'clock Hélène and Mademoiselle Rose went out. It was rare for shots to be fired at that time of day, so the streets were quiet.

They could see a lamp that had accidentally been left on at the back of an abandoned house whose windows were nailed shut with planks of wood. The fog filled Hélène's mouth and slipped down into her throat; it tasted heavy and sickly. That day, as they walked along, Hélène suddenly took hold of Mademoiselle Rose's hand, shyly squeezed it and held on to her slim fingers in their black wool gloves.

'Mademoiselle Rose . . .'

Mademoiselle Rose shuddered, but said nothing and let go of Hélène's hand, as if that physical contact had inter-rupted some faraway sound, a sound that she, and she alone, could hear. Hélène sighed and fell silent. The air was ashen and grew thicker with every passing moment. At times, the street was so dark that Mademoiselle Rose became a shadowy figure lost in the mist; Hélène stretched out her hand in anguish and felt for her coat; then they continued walking, in silence. Every now and again a street lamp, lit as if by some miracle, cast its cloudy light over them, and in the opaque air, beneath a flickering mist, she could see Mademoiselle Rose's thin face, her pursed little mouth, her black velvet hat. In the darkness they could smell the rancid odour of the canals; no one had bothered to clean them since the February Revolution; no one bothered to repair their stones; the city was crumbling beneath the weight of the water, slowly disintegrating, becoming a city of smoke, illusions and fog, retreating into a void.

'I'm tired,' said Hélène. 'I want to go home.'

Mademoiselle Rose said nothing. Yet even though she let out no sound, it seemed as if her lips had moved. In any case the fog muffled everyone's voices.

They continued walking.

'It must be late,' thought Hélène.

She was hungry.

'What time is it?' she asked.

No reply. She wanted to look at her wristwatch but it was too dark. They passed by the large clock at the Winter Palace; Hélène slowed down to try to hear it ringing, but Mademoiselle Rose kept on walking; Hélène had to run to catch up with her. She later remembered that the clock was broken and no longer chimed.

The fog had suddenly become so thick that she was finding it difficult to keep up with Mademoiselle Rose. But the street was very narrow; she soon caught hold of the familiar woollen coat. 'Wait for me, won't you; you're walking so fast . . . I'm tired; I want to go home.'

She waited for a reply, in vain.

'I want to go home,' she said again, sounding frightened and upset.

Then, suddenly, she stopped, frozen, as Mademoiselle Rose started talking to herself, quietly, sensibly. 'It's late, but the house is quite close by. Why haven't they lit the lamps? Mama never forgets to put a lamp on the window ledge when it starts getting dark. That's where we sit, my sisters and I, to sew and read. Did you know that Marcel is back?' she said, turning to Hélène. 'He'll find you've grown so much. Do you remember the day that he carried you on his back to climb the tower of Notre-Dame? You laughed and laughed . . . You don't laugh very often any more, you poor little thing. Listen, I knew I shouldn't get attached to you, I was warned about it. By whom? I forget. You should never get attached to other people's children. I could have had a child of my own. He'd be your age now, I wanted to throw myself into the Seine. It was love, you see . . . but no, I'm old . . . You do understand that I have to go home, Hélène. I'm very tired . . . My sisters are waiting for me. I'll see my little Marcel . . .'

She gave a mocking laugh that turned into a painful sigh. Then she said a few disjointed words, but she sounded calmer, more matter-of-fact. She had taken Hélène's hand again and squeezed it tightly. Hélène followed her; all of this seemed so strange to her that she had the feeling of being in a deep trance. They crossed one of the bridges over the Neva decorated by leaping horses; their bronze backs were covered in fine, light snow. Hélène's hand brushed against the statue's pedestal as she walked by and the snow fell down on her, covering her coat; once again she heard the mad little laugh that ended in a sigh. The fog descended suddenly once more.

Mademoiselle Rose hurried on. 'Keep up,' she kept saying impatiently, 'walk faster . . .'

The street was empty. A lone sailor emerged from the shadows at the corner of a grand building; he had a gold snuffbox in his hand that he pushed under Hélène's nose; she could clearly see the dark stains of blackish blood he had neglected to wipe off, so they remained on the gold cover; the man seemed to have only half a body, to be floating in the fog that hid his legs and the top of his head; then a cloud of smoke rose between him and Hélène and he disappeared into the night.

'Stop!' Hélène cried in despair. 'Let go of me. I want to go home!'

Mademoiselle Rose shuddered and lessened her grip. Hélène could hear her give a quiet sigh. When she next spoke her delirium seemed to have passed. 'Don't be afraid, Lili,' she said softly. 'We're going home now. I haven't been able to remember things for quite a while now. There was a light over there, at the end of the street that reminded me of the house. You wouldn't understand . . . But now, alas, I remember that was all in the past. I wonder if it's the sound of gunfire that's doing this to me. You can hear it all night long outside our windows. You're asleep, but at my age the nights are long.'

She fell silent, then said anxiously, 'Can't you hear the cries?'

'No, no . . . let's go home, faster. You're ill.'

They weren't sure where they were. Hélène was shivering with the cold; every now and again she thought she recognised a street or a monument through the fog; a tall statue on its pedestal appeared in the mist; they were drawing closer to the Neva, but the fog was getting heavier and heavier; they had to hold on to the walls as they walked.

'If only you'd listened to me,' Hélène said angrily. 'Now we're lost . . .'

But Mademoiselle Rose walked with strange rapidity and blind confidence; out of habit Hélène held on to her governess's otter-skin muff with its artificial violets sewn on to the fur.

'Do you recognise this road? I can't see a thing. Mademoiselle Rose! Answer me! What are you thinking about?'

'What are you saying, Lili? Talk louder, I can't hear you . . .'

'The fog is muffling our voices . . .'

'The fog and the cries. It's funny that you can't hear the cries . . . They're far away, very far away, but so clear . . . Are you tired, my poor darling? But that doesn't matter, it doesn't matter, let's hurry up, hurry up,' she said again anxiously.

'Oh, but why?' Hélène said bitterly. 'It's not as if anyone is waiting for us. *They* couldn't care less. *She's* with her Max. Oh, how I hate her . . .'

'Now, now!' Mademoiselle Rose said quietly. 'You mustn't say that. It isn't nice . . .'

She started walking again extremely quickly.

'But where are you going?' Hélène asked. 'Think for a moment. You can't even see. I'm sure we're getting further and further away from the house.'

'I know where I'm going,' Mademoiselle Rose said impatiently. 'Don't worry about it. Follow me. We'll soon be able to rest.'

Suddenly she pulled her hand free, leaving Hélène holding the muff; she took a few steps forward, must have turned at the corner of the street and was immediately engulfed by the fog; she disappeared like a ghost, like a dream.

Hélène rushed after her, shouting, 'Wait for me, I'm begging you! Where are you going? You'll get yourself killed!

There's gunfire on that side of the road! Oh, wait for me, wait for me, I beg you. I'm afraid! You're going to get hurt!'

She could see nothing; the fog was all around her; she thought she could make out a shape in the distance; she rushed towards it, but it was a soldier who pushed her aside.

'Help!' she cried. 'Help me! Did you see a woman go by here?'

But the soldier was drunk and a child's voice begging for help was common in those times. He walked away, holding on to the walls. Then she thought she had perhaps run too fast, that Mademoiselle Rose's weak legs wouldn't have been able to take her this far; she retraced her steps; she was walking through a thick fog that rolled in as slowly as smoke, every now and again revealing the outline of a large house set high on a hill, a street lamp or the arch of a bridge before immediately hiding them again.

'I'll never find her,' she thought in despair, 'never.'

Her own voice sounded weak, muffled by the mist. 'Mademoiselle Rose, oh dear, dear Mademoiselle Rose. Wait for me, answer me. Where are you?'

She could see a light faintly glimmering; she leaned forward; some men were standing around a dead horse; they were cutting it up in silence, bit by bit; a hand held up a lantern; right in front of her, the man's long, yellowish teeth stood out in the darkness as he gave a hollow laugh. Hélène let out a cry and rushed down a strange street that ran between some large houses. She was panting; with each step she could feel the sharp pain that accompanied her every breath; she had no idea where she was; she recognised nothing; she was lost, terrified amid the clouds of fog; she fled far away from the men, from the sinister lamplight, from the long jaws of death. Every now and again she would cry out, 'Help, help me! Mademoiselle Rose!'

But her weak, breathless voice immediately faded away. Besides, calling for help in those days only made the rare passers-by rush faster towards their homes. She was still running. She spotted a street lamp in the distance, for there was one in every road; it gave off a pale light, surrounded by a reddish halo and only lit up a bit of dark ground and the rolling fog; she ran towards it, leaping through the darkness; she leaned against the street lamp, panting, hugging its bronze column covered in damp snow as if it were the living body of a friend. She held some snow in her hands; the icy contact calmed her down. She looked around desperately for another human being, but there was no one. The street was deserted. She turned in circles round the same tall houses, lost in the fog, always ending up back at the same place. At one point she bumped into a passer-by, but when she smelled his breath against her face, saw his strange, wild eyes looking her up and down, she felt as if her heart would stop beating out of terror; it took all her strength to free herself from his grip and run away again, far away, clenching her teeth and calling out, 'Mademoiselle Rose! Where are you, where are you? Mademoiselle Rose!'

But deep down inside she was certain that she would never see her again. She finally stopped, whispering in despair, 'I have to get home now, try to get home . . . Perhaps she's at the house?'

She then remembered that, in any case, Mademoiselle Rose would soon be leaving.

'If she has to die,' she said out loud, hearing the words coming from her lips with painful surprise, 'if it's her time . . . My God, perhaps it's better this way . . .'

Tears were streaming down her face; she felt that because she had stopped fighting destiny she had abandoned Mademoiselle Rose to her fate. She was walking along the quayside now; she could feel the granite of the stone walls against her hands; it was wet and icy; she was shivering from the cold; the wind had picked up and filled the air with an angry sound.

The smell of the water, that rotting odour of the canals in St Petersburg, which to her was the very breath of the city, suddenly lifted; the fog wafted away, rolled slowly far from her. She stood and looked at the water in the canal for a long time. 'I'd happily throw myself in,' she thought, 'I want to die.'

But she knew very well that she was lying. Everything she could see at that moment, everything she felt, her own unhappiness, her solitude and this dark water, the little flames from the gaslights flickering in the wind, everything, right down to her feeling of despair, drove her to choose life.

She stopped and slowly wiped her forehead. 'No, I won't let them do it to me,' she said out loud. 'I'm brave . . .'

She forced herself to look at the water, to overcome the troubling pull of its pulsating currents; she took deep breaths, tasting the wind.

'At least I have that,' she thought. 'I'm horrid, hard-hearted, I don't know how to forgive, but I'm courageous. My God! Help me!'

And slowly, clenching her teeth to stop herself from crying, she found her way home.

# 6

Mademoiselle Rose died that night in hospital; some soldiers had carried her there, for she had fainted on a street corner. A letter she had in her coat pocket, the last letter she'd received from France, was used to identify her from the name on the envelope.

The Karols were informed. She hadn't suffered, they told Hélène. Her tired heart had stopped beating. She'd had a fit of delirium, presumably because she was homesick . . . She must have been ill for a long time.

'You poor thing,' said Hélène's mother. 'She was so attached to you. We would have given her a modest pension and she would have lived a quiet life. Although she might have felt very alone, because we're leaving and we couldn't have taken her with us. Perhaps it's for the best.'

However, so many people were dying that no one, not then and not later, had time to waste on consoling Hélène. 'Poor little thing,' they said. 'Just imagine how frightened she must have been. I hope she doesn't get sick. That's all we need . . .'

The day came to an end and Hélène found herself alone in her empty room, surrounded by the dead woman's personal things: the old photograph of her with her sisters when she was twenty, so faded you could barely see it; her fine hair framed her face like a wisp of smoke; she wore a velvet ribbon round her neck and a belt with a buckle round her slim waist. Hélène studied the photo for a long time. She didn't cry. She felt as if the weight of her tears filled her heart, making it as hard and heavy as stone.

They were due to depart in two days' time. They were going to Finland. Karol would take them there and then come back to collect the gold ingots he'd left with a friend in Moscow. Max was leaving with them. His mother and sisters had fled to the Caucasus but he refused to join them. Karol looked the other way. Hélène heard her parents in the next room; they were sorting through Bella's jewellery and sewing it into their clothing. She could hear their muffled whispering and the clinking of gold.

'If only I'd known,' thought Hélène. 'If only I'd understood that the poor woman was going mad, I could have told the grown-ups. They would have taken care of her, made her well again, she'd still be alive . . .'

But then she immediately shook her head with a sad little snigger. Who, for God's sake, would have had the time to take care of her? What was the health and life of a human being worth these days? What did it matter whether one person lived and the other died? All over the city people carried dead children to the cemetery tied up in sacks, for there were simply too many to afford a coffin. A few days before, during a break between lessons, she herself had watched a man being executed; and she was just a little girl in a smock, with fat curls round her neck and fingers stained with ink; she stood glued to the window, staring out, without looking away, without crying out, with no outward sign of emotion except for a gradual draining of colour in her face until her lips turned white. Five soldiers were lined up opposite a wounded man who stood against a wall, his head bandaged and bloody, swaying as if he were drunk. He fell to the ground; they carried him away, just as on another day they had carried away some dead woman on a stretcher, wrapped in her black shawl, just as a starving dog had come to die beneath that very window, his emaciated body cut open and bleeding. And the child returned to her desk and mumbled her way through her lesson by the faint light of a candle: 'Racine depicts men as they are, and Corneille as they should be . . .'

Or: 'The father of our current beloved Emperor, Nicholas II, was called Alexander III and ascended to the throne in . . .' for the history books hadn't yet been updated.

Life, death, they were so insignificant . . .

Her heavy head fell down on to her chest, but what she feared most was sleep. She didn't want to fall asleep, didn't want to forget, didn't want to wake up when her consciousness of unhappiness was still only vague and hazy, and look around for that familiar face in the other empty bed . . .

She clenched her teeth, looked out into the night, but the darkness was terrifying, full of sneering faces and swirls of black water, or so it seemed. The fog clung to the windows with its pale mist, lit up by the moon. The dank smell of water seemed to seep through the closed windows, rising up from the street, slithering towards her. And when it filled her with horror, she would turn away and see the empty bed once more.

'Go on,' a voice within her whispered, 'call your parents, they're here, they'll understand that you're afraid, they'll let you sleep somewhere else, they'll take away that other bed, so flat, so empty . . .'

But she wanted at least to hold on to her pride.

'What am I, a child? Am I afraid of death, of unhappiness? Afraid of being alone? No, I won't call for anyone and certainly not for them. I don't need them. I'm stronger than all of them. They won't see me cry. They aren't worthy of helping me. I'll never say her name again, never. They aren't worthy of hearing it.'

The next day it was Hélène who sorted out the chest of drawers and put Mademoiselle Rose's meagre belongings into a trunk; it was she who packed away the linen, then the books, then the blouses whose every pleat, every careful stitch were so familiar, then the coat that had been returned to them, still steeped in the smell of fog. She closed the lid, turned the key and never again spoke the name of Mademoiselle Rose in front of her family.

# PART III

# 1

The sleigh rushed towards a faint light that seemed to disappear then return, happily twinkling through the falling
snow. The night was crystal clear and bitterly cold. The
snowfields of Finland were endless, without a single rock,
a single hill, just an enormous expanse of ice as far as the
eye could see; at the horizon the ice seemed to curve slightly,
as if it were embracing the entire world.

Hélène had left St Petersburg that morning. It was only
the beginning of November, but here it was already the dead
of winter. There was no wind, but an icy mist blew joyously
from the ground, rushing towards the dark sky, towards the
stars, making them flicker like candles in a breeze. For a while
the stars looked duller, glimmering like mirrors when you
breathe on them; but when the freezing mist dissolved they
shone even more brightly and the snow took on a kind of
bluish glow that seemed very close by. All you had to do
was reach out and touch it . . . the horses were catching it
up and you could grab it in your hand. But no, the sleigh

continued on its way and the faint sparkle disappeared, then returned to shimmer, mockingly.

There was a turning in the road; the light on the horizon grew brighter; the horses shook the rows of little bells hanging from their necks so that each one rang out more joyously. Hélène felt the rushing wind whistle past her ears, then the horses slowed down again and the little bells became soft and languid once more.

Hélène was sitting between her parents and opposite Max, at the back of the sleigh. She leaned forward and opened the shawl that covered her face to breathe in the air slowly, as if it were ice-cold wine. For three years she had only smelled the faint odour of rotting water in St Petersburg; now she rediscovered the pleasure of feeling clean air flow freely into her nostrils, her open mouth, deep into her entire body, right down to her heart, she felt, her heart that beat with more strength and vigour.

Karol stretched out his hand and pointed to the light that was getting closer. 'That must be the place, don't you think?'

A lump of snow flew away from beneath the horses' hooves and Hélène could smell the scent of pine trees, ice, earth and wind that seemed the very breath of the north, never to be forgotten. 'This is nice,' she thought.

They were getting closer; they could see it now. It was a simple two-storey house made of wood. A gate covered in snow creaked open.

'Well, here we are!' said Karol. 'I'll just have a glass of vodka and get going.'

'What? Right now?' cried Bella, her voice quivering with joy.

'Yes,' he said. 'I have to. It would be dangerous to wait. The border could be closed at any moment.'

'But what's going to happen to us?' Bella protested.

He leaned forward and kissed her. But Hélène had seen none of this. She had leapt down and was joyously stamping her feet on ground; it was as hard and shiny as a diamond. She breathed in the icy, clean air of the winter's night; a bright reddish fire glistened through a window; the sound of a waltz echoed through the empty landscape.

Hélène felt a kind of serenity and profound peace that she had never before experienced in her short life. And immediately afterwards a childlike exhilaration, a sort of joyous passion that filled her soul, the way drinking a tonic is followed by a sense of well-being. She ran into the house. Her parents stood with their friends on the doorstep. Through the open door she could vaguely make out what they were saying:

'The Revolution . . . The Reds . . . It will last all winter, at the very least . . .'

'There are no troubles here . . .'

'Lambs, sheep, that's what the Communists are around here,' a man proclaimed loudly. 'May God protect them. And we have butter, flour, eggs . . .'

'There's no flour,' a woman said, 'you mustn't exaggerate. As far as I'm concerned, if they told me there was any flour left in heaven, I wouldn't believe it.'

Hélène heard them laugh; she went into the hall where, later on, she would so often stop to take off her ice skates; she could see the dining room through the open door. It was a kind of canteen with a large table set for twenty people. The floors, walls and furniture were all made of the same light, shiny wood, which gave off the delicious smell of freshly cut pine trees whose sap flows through a groove deep in the heart of their trunks. But what struck Hélène most was the joyful sound that filled the entire house; she heard children shouting, young voices, sounds she had forgotten existed. Children came in from outside, groups of them, gangs of them, carrying their sledges on their shoulders, their ice skates hanging from their necks by the laces, their cheeks bright red from the cold night air, their hair powdered with snow. Hélène glanced scornfully at them. She was much older than they were. She was fifteen. She shook her head and sighed like an old woman. It had come upon her so quickly, at such a sad time, this age she had dreamed of being, in Nice, when she was little, when Mademoiselle Rose was still alive . . . A wave of pain rose in her heart. She took a few steps, opened a door, saw a shabby little sitting room where some young women were dancing. They looked at Hélène coldly. She went back into the hall where two little boys with blond hair and fat rosy cheeks were playing.

A young man, his shoulders covered with snow, appeared on the doorstep. The children shouted 'Papa!' and ran towards him; he took them in his arms. A very beautiful woman opened a door and smiled; she had a calm face and black hair held neatly in place by a headband.

'Good Lord, Fred, just look at you!' she said with mocking affection. 'Let go of the children, you'll get snow all over them.'

The young man shook himself free and laughed; he removed his fur hat, noticed Hélène and smiled at her. Then he walked over to his wife, who took his arm. A servant came to fetch the children; they hung off their mother's skirt, a full, wide, black taffeta skirt that rustled softly. She leaned down to kiss them. Hélène noticed her long gold earrings with pearls at the ends that sparkled against her dark hair. She had beautiful hands with no jewellery and wore a pleated linen collar. She sensed Hélène was staring at her and gave her a smile. Then her husband opened the door and they disappeared. Hélène could hear the heavy silk dress swishing and the sound of the piano as it echoed through the house; the woman began singing a French love song in a warm, soft voice. Hélène stood very still, listening, lost in happy thoughts. She barely heard her father calling her: he was leaving. She ran towards him; he kissed her with the restrained, defiant affection that was the only emotion he allowed himself to show her; the sleigh that had brought them was waiting in front of the house; he sat down in the back and was gone.

Hélène rushed into the garden. She ran around it, panting and breathing in the snow. The frozen white path beneath her feet glistened faintly, lit up by a lamp near the steps. What a joy it was to run like this. Her legs were already womanly but had lost none of their agility. The dinner bell rang. The simple fact of this delightful, calming routine filled Hélène with extraordinary pleasure. The shabby little piano sent the notes of the ballad ringing into the still night while the tender voice rose effortlessly, like the song of a bird, like an arrow, up towards the icy sky.

A big yellow dog came out of the darkness and put his wet nose in Hélène's hand. She hugged him and gave him a kiss. She could smell hot soup and cakes made of the potato flour they had to use instead of ordinary flour.

'I'm hungry,' she thought and ran back towards the house.

Even this hunger was a new sensation for her, different from the nagging, odious need to eat she'd felt in St Petersburg when food, though still available, was getting harder and harder to come by. She walked around the house, looked at the glowing stove, the lit lamp, a woman in a white apron standing by the light of the fire . . . How peaceful everything was! Once again she thought of Mademoiselle Rose, but the memory of her, despite being so recent, had already begun to fade. This was surely because it was so tragic: in Hélène's mind it was transformed into a kind of mournful, poetic dream. In spite of herself she felt carefree, distant, light, free; she was ashamed, but thought, 'Now that the poor woman is gone, nothing *they* can do will ever be able to hurt me.'

She went back to stand beneath the windows of the little sitting room, enjoying the sensation of wading through the hard, thick snow that crunched softly. A lamp covered in a piece of red cloth lit up the room. The woman in black who had called out 'Fred!' was now quietly playing a waltz. Her young husband leaned in towards her and kissed her shoulder. A feeling of mysterious poetry, of sweet exhilaration, rushed through Hélène. She jumped off the pile of snow where she sat perched, and they must have seen her little silhouette disappear into the night. The woman leaned forward and smiled; the young man laughed, then shook his finger at her. She ran away, her heart pounding joyously, laughing quietly, for no reason, simply out of pleasure at hearing the forgotten sound of laughter echo through the night.

# 2

The border had not yet been closed, but every train seemed as if it would be the last. Each trip to St Petersburg was an amazing feat, an act of madness and courage. Yet Bella Karol and Max went back every week on some different pretext, for they were never as happy anywhere as in the empty house in St Petersburg: Boris Karol was stuck in Moscow, unable to get away. The Safronovs had left the Caucasus, but Max didn't know whether they had managed to reach Persia or Constantinople. At the beginning of December he received a letter from his mother begging him to come to her, saying she was alone, old and ill, complaining that he had abandoned her 'for that horrible woman'. 'She'll be your undoing,' she wrote. 'Be careful. I'll die without ever seeing you again. You love me, Max. You won't forgive yourself for ignoring how I'm begging you. Come back to me, do everything you can to come back to me.'

But he had delayed his departure until finally it was impossible to cross southern Russia, as it was occupied by the White Army. The day he learned this he had gone into

Bella's room. Ignoring Hélène, who was also there, he said, 'I have a feeling that I'm never going to see my family again. You're all I have left in the world.'

When they went to St Petersburg, Max and Bella left Hélène behind, vaguely relying on others to look after her, in particular Zenia Reuss, the young woman she'd seen that first evening, and an elderly woman named Madame Haas, who said, when talking about Bella, 'That creature a mother? The caricature of a mother more like!'

Several different groups of people lived together in Finland; they were on good terms with each other, like passengers caught in a storm, bonding regardless of social class or wealth: Russians, Jews who came from 'good families' (the ones who spoke English together and followed the rites of their religion with proud humility), and the nouveaux riches, sceptics, free thinkers with masses of money.

In the evening they all gathered in the shabby little sitting room. The card players sat round a bridge table; they were always the same people: the fat Salomon Levy with his pot belly and scarlet neck, the Baron and Baroness Lennart, Russians of Swedish origin who were both tall, thin, pale and half hidden in a cloud of their own cigarette smoke. The Baron had a soft, hushed voice and the affected, gentle laugh of a young girl, while his wife spoke with the harshness of a grenadier; she told risqué stories, drank a small decanter of brandy every night, but automatically crossed herself every time the Lord's name was spoken, without pausing for breath.

Madame Haas's elderly husband was also there, a blanket thrown over his shoulders: a fragile man with a weak heart, he had a bluish puffy swelling under his eyes, the sign of the slow death eating away at his flesh. He played cards while his wife sat next to him, gazing at him with the look of anxiety, hope and bad temper unique to people responsible for caring for someone they love who is terminally ill; occasionally she would look away, briskly lifting her head above her pearl 'dog collar' and aiming her lorgnette at anyone in sight. The servants lit the gas lamps. The young women sat on uncomfortable little bamboo settees, flimsy and creaky, embroidering doilies. Madame Reuss was one of them. When the other women talked about her they said, 'She's beautiful . . .'

After a moment of silence they added, 'She has a charming husband . . .'

Then they would slowly shake their heads and with a spontaneous, indulgent smile hovering on their lips and the secretive, proud, scandalised, hypocritical expression of women who know more than they are saying, they would murmur, 'That Fred, he's such a devil . . .'

Fred Reuss was thirty years old yet looked extraordinarily young; he had shining, playful dark eyes, a lively, mischievous expression and white teeth. Just like the children, he never sat still, always ready to leap up, skip away, never able simply to walk round a chair if he could jump over it, running and playing in the snow with his sons, while his calm, serious, beautiful wife watched him and smiled with maternal tenderness. Fred Reuss only seemed serious when he looked at his eldest son, his one love. He attended to no one's needs, dodged all his responsibilities, avoided any type of suffering by making light of the situation, or laughing, or doing a little dance. His laughter burst forth, as irresistible as a child's. His teasing was subtle and mischievous. With all women, and especially his wife, he played at being the spoiled child;

even Madame Haas liked him. Joy followed him wherever he went. He was one of those men who seem eternally young, who don't know how to mature, but who will suddenly grow old, become bitter, spiteful and tyrannical. But for now he was still young.

And so the evenings passed. The children hung on to the maids' arms and aprons as they took them up to bed. A damp mist gradually covered the icy windows; the lamp glimmered, giving off smoke.

The Jews talked about business and, either to amuse themselves or to keep in practice, sold each other land, mines and houses even though the Bolsheviks had confiscated them months earlier. But to consider this type of government as here to stay would have been a sign of bad faith. They thought it would only last for two or three months. The pessimists conceded it might last through the winter. They also speculated on the rouble, the Finnish mark and the Swedish crown. The rates were so unpredictable that in the space of a week, the dark, shabby little sitting room with its soft velvet and bamboo furniture saw fortunes made and lost, while outside the snow continued to fall.

The Russians would listen, haughty, defiant, then intrigued, interested; they moved their chairs in a bit closer. At the end of the evening they would affectionately put their arms round the necks of the men they had, until then, referred to as 'Israelites'.

Among themselves they would even say, 'Really, they've been maligned. Some of them are charming.'

The Jews would say, 'They're far from being as stupid as people make out. The prince would have made an excellent stockbroker if he'd needed to earn his living.'

And so the two opposing races lived side by side, thrown together by the hardship of the times. And because they were linked by self-interest, habit and adversity, they were all part of the same little society, united and happy.

The smoke from the fat cigars rose slowly into the air; stacks of banknotes, whose value fell every day, were scattered around the floor; no one bothered to pick them up and they were often ripped up by the dogs. Sometimes people would go outside to stand on the terrace covered in crunchy snow and watch the faint light of fires burning in the distance.

'Terrioki is burning,' they would say indifferently, then go back inside, shaking off the snow that in an instant had covered their shoulders and backs.

Meanwhile, music from the little black piano rang out beneath the fingers of a tall, thin young girl with flaxen hair; she had tuberculosis and looked fragile and worn out; she spent every day on the terrace, motionless in her fur wrap and, when evening fell, she would walk across it, without stopping, without answering the friendly questions she was asked, as if she were a night owl, both attracted and frightened by the light from the living room; sitting herself down on the small green velvet piano stool, she would play continuously, moving from a Chopin nocturne to a rondo by Handel to a Ta-ra-ra-boom-diay, her cheeks burning from the fever she had every night.

The young women taught Hélène how to sew and embroider; she felt content, happy; she rediscovered the health and vigour of her childhood; the snow, the wind, the long races through the forest had returned the passionate pink glow to her cheeks; she sometimes cast a furtive, shy glance at herself in the mirror and smiled.

'How that little girl is changing!' the women said, looking at her affectionately. 'She looks so healthy.'

For the moment Hélène preferred the company of this group of wise women who listened with pursed lips to Baroness Lennart, talked among themselves about their children and exchanged recipes for jam; while the glow of fires burning in the distance grew brighter through the windows, they bent their heads under the lamplight and cut delicate holes in linen doilies with little gold scissors.

On Saturday evenings they would go to the village to watch the servants and the Red Guards dance. They climbed into wide, rural sleighs lined with furs or sheepskins. It was impossible to sit up; they stretched out, leaning on one elbow, and fell on top of one another every time they hit a bump.

Madame Reuss stayed at home with the younger children, but her husband wouldn't have missed one of the 'balls' for the world. He brought his eldest son George with him, but would then leave him in the care of the elderly Madame Haas in order to come and lie beside Hélène. Smiling, he tried to hold her hand in the darkness; he would gently slip off her rough wool glove and squeeze her thin fingers that trembled imperceptibly. Hélène, her heart pounding, looked at the face leaning in towards hers, lit up by the moonlight and the misty, flickering flame of the smoking lantern that hung at the side of the sleigh. An ironic, affectionate little smile hovered on Fred's lips, on his feminine, quivering mouth; the snow settled on the fur blanket like sequins, bright little sparkling stars. Hélène closed her eyes; she was tired; she had run and played all day in the snow; when they had no toboggans, they used a sleigh with no brakes to hurtle down the hill at great speed; it always seemed to hit some frozen rock, throwing everyone into the thick, soft snow in the deep undergrowth of the forest. Hélène had rediscovered her love of dangerous games, the tomboy rough and tumble.

The dances on Saturday evenings took place in a barn whose roof was poorly constructed so you could see the dark sky dimly illuminated by the faint flickering of the stars, just like in a Christmas Nativity scene. The musicians straddled benches and played noisy fanfares on drums and brass instruments; the boys danced with loaded guns and large hunting knives with wide flat blades sheathed in stag skin that rattled in their belts as they stamped their boots on the floor. Every now and again a strong-smelling cloud of dust flew up, made of bits of hay, for the storerooms were below the floor; the girls wore red smocks and, to emphasise they were Loyalists, scarlet ribbons in their blond hair and red petticoats beneath their dresses that showed when they danced.

Sometimes the door would open and an icy wind would rush through the room. From the doorstep they could see the pine trees lit up by the moon; they were tall, still, silvery, and every branch was frozen, as hard and sparkling as steel, glimmering through the darkness. The wood-burning stove hummed; they fed it with newly cut logs, still damp and coated with snow. Thick smoke filled the room, mingling with the mist formed by the dancers' breath and the steam that rose from the greatcoats and fur hats. Hélène sat on a wooden table, swinging her feet; Fred Reuss stood opposite her and squeezed her leg hard. Hélène pulled away, but behind her a couple was kissing so passionately that they were almost lying on the table. She sat forward again, leaning towards the young man; silently she drank in this new joy, the peace and warmth in her heart that came from the feel of Fred's body as he gently caressed her ankle. She basked in the new, confusing pleasure of holding her face in such a way that the light fell on to her cheek, for she knew that it was smooth and flawless, aflame with the burning, passionate blood of youth. She laughed in order to show off her white, shiny teeth; she let Fred press her swarthy, thin little hand between his body and the table. The gas lamps hanging from the roof were filled with yellow oil; they swung about when the dancing started up again; it was a kind of French folk dance that finished with some fast turns, which made the floorboards creak and groan. In Reuss's arms, Hélène skipped and spun round; her face was pale, her lips pinched; she felt her soul fill with gentle dizziness. All around her the ribbons and long hair of the girls flew by, whipping their cheeks, lashing Hélène's face when the dancing couples hurtled into one another.

When the men had danced enough and had their fill of contraband alcohol, they picked up their Mausers and shot bullets into the roof. Standing on the table, both hands holding on to Reuss's shoulders, digging her nails into his back in excitement without even realising it, Hélène watched this game, breathing in the smell of gunpowder that she already knew so well. Reuss's eldest son, his head as closely shaven as a lawn in spring, jumped joyously up and down on the spot in his coat and twill shirt. It was only when there were no more bullets left that the scuffles began.

'Come on, we have to go now,' Fred Reuss said with regret. 'Whatever will my wife say? It's nearly midnight, come quickly now . . .'

They left; outside, the horses were waiting, sniffing the

frozen earth, every now and again shaking the snow from their heads; the little bells they wore round their necks would swing, and a sweet, mysterious ringing sound swept through the forest and over the river in its icy shell. Hélène and Reuss, half asleep, swayed gently to the rhythm of the horses' gait as they climbed the hill. Hélène felt her cheeks burning as if they were on fire; the long day, her tiredness and the smoke made her eyelids feel heavy; she looked lazily up at the pink moon as it slowly rose in the winter sky.

# 3

Hélène whistled for the dogs, silently opened the gate and went out into the garden. The sky was pale and bright; not a single bird could be heard singing in the countryside; between the sparse pine trees, tracks in the shape of stars marked the thick snow where animals had passed by; the dogs sniffed the ground; then they ran off towards the woods where, every day for more than a week, Hélène and Reuss had been meeting.

At first he had come with his sons, then alone. At the edge of the woods stood an abandoned house; it was a former dacha, a holiday home made of wood, painted eau-de-nil, with entrance steps guarded by two stone griffons; it looked as if it had been set on fire, but then the fire had been put out: one entire section of wall was blackened by smoke. Stones thrown at the windows had shattered them: standing on tiptoe, you could see into a dark sitting room full of furniture. One day Reuss had reached in through one of the windows and pulled out a photograph in a frame that had been hanging on the wall. The picture was all crinkly and yellow beneath the glass, probably because of the dampness of the long autumn and winter with no fire lit. It was a photograph of a woman. They studied it for a long time, feeling uneasy; the features of the mysterious woman evoked a vague, sombre sense of the poetic. Then they buried the photograph in the snow, beneath a fir tree. The doors of the house had come loose and swayed on their half-broken hinges.

On that day, while waiting for Hélène, Reuss had gone into the barn and taken a few lightweight Finnish sledges from among the heap of things there. They were made of simple garden chairs set on to blades. The backs of the chairs still bore children's names carved into the wood with a penknife in large, clumsy letters. Whenever anyone asked the farmers in the area what had happened to the people who'd lived in the house, they suddenly seemed not to understand Russian, or any other language. They would screw up their cruel narrow eyes and turn away without replying.

As Hélène wandered through the house, drawn to it by its overwhelming sense of abandonment and sadness, Fred Reuss came up to her and pulled her hair. 'Leave it be!' He laughed. 'It smells old, miserable and dead. Come with me, young lady.' He pointed towards the icy road that went down a little incline on to a plain. 'Let's go!'

The Finnish sledges were steered by skaters who stood behind the chair in which the other person sat. But this was too slow for Hélène's and Reuss's liking; they both climbed on to the back and launched the sledge into the snow. It went rushing down the hill, faster and faster; the wind blew into their ears, burning them harshly.

'Be careful, be careful!' cried Fred and his joyous laughter rang out in the clear icy air. 'Careful! The tree! The rock! We're falling! We're going to die! Hold on tight, Hélène. Stamp your foot against the ground. Like this. Again. Again! Faster . . . Oh, this is so wonderful.'

Gasping for breath, they slid silently along with the dizzying speed you feel in a dream, down the long hill, along the icy white path on to the plain. They kept on going until the sledge hit a tree stump and threw its passengers into the snow. Ten times, a hundred times, they started over again, never tiring, hauling the sledge up to the top, then sliding down the long, icy hill.

Hélène could feel the young man's hot breath against her neck; the biting cold made tears run down her face but she couldn't wipe them away: as they sped along, the wind dried them on her cheeks. They both shouted out with joy as they stamped on the frozen ground, shrieking like children, without even realising it. The little sledge shot forward, hurtling down the hill like an arrow.

'Listen,' Fred said after a while, 'it's not going fast enough. What we need is a real sledge.'

'How can we get one?' asked Hélène. 'The last time we smashed it up and ever since the driver is careful to lock up the shed. But I saw one there in the barn . . .'

They ran back to the barn and took the most beautiful sledge they could find; it was lined in red, with a little row of bells hanging from its sides. They had some difficulty getting it going, but once it started picking up speed, nothing in the world could go as fast; the snow flew into their faces, into their panting, half-open mouths, blinding them, whipping their cheeks. Hélène couldn't see a thing. The brilliant whiteness of the plain was dazzling beneath the sharp reddish winter sun that cast a scarlet glow on to the snow. Little by little, though, it grew paler, turned pink.

'This is so thrilling,' thought Hélène.

They stopped counting how many times they flew down the hill. Finally, after they were thrown into a ravine and barely made it out, their cheeks scratched by the icy pine needles, Reuss, who laughed until he cried, said, 'We're going to crack our heads open, that's for sure! Let's go back to the calm little Finnish sledge.'

'Never! Rolling around in the snow is the best part.'

'Ah, really? So that's what you like the most?' murmured Reuss. He pulled her towards him and held her tightly against him for a moment. He seemed to hesitate; she stood pressed against him, looking at him with her joyful eyes that had rediscovered all their innocence.

'Well then, if you like rolling around in the snow,' he said suddenly, 'climb on to my shoulders.'

He grabbed her round the waist, helped her perch on his shoulders, then threw her into the deep snow two feet in front of him. She shouted with pleasure and fear; she plunged into the snow as if it were a feathered nest; snow ran down her neck through a gap in her sweater; it got inside her gloves, filled her mouth with the icy sweet taste of sorbet. Hélène's heart pounded with happiness. She looked with anguish at the early dusk sweeping across the sky.

'We're not going home yet, are we? We can stay a while longer, can't we?' she begged. 'It's not dark yet . . .'

'We do have to go home,' said Fred with regret.

She stood up, shook herself off and they walked back up the road. In the field of snow, only a single band of light remained and darkness fell strangely quickly; it was a soft, lilac colour; in the luminous sky the pale winter moon rose slowly above a frozen little lake. They didn't speak. Their footsteps echoed over the frozen earth. Far, far away in the distance, they heard the muted sound of a cannon. They only half listened to it. For months now the low rumbling was so constant that they had stopped hearing it. But where was it coming from? Who was firing? Whom were they firing at? When faced with a certain level of horror the human mind becomes saturated and reacts with indifference and egotism. They walked side by side, tired and happy. Hélène could feel Reuss staring at her. Suddenly he stopped and took her face in his hands. He brought her cheek closer to his, seemed to look in astonishment for a moment at its smoothness, at the hint of red, so warm and passionate rising up to her skin, and breathed in her face as if it were a rose; the kiss was hesitant, settling in the middle of her half-open lips, a swift, gentle kiss as passionate as fire. Her first kiss, the first time a man's lips had ever touched hers this way.

Her initial reaction was one of fear and anger. 'What are you doing?' she cried. 'Are you mad?'

She picked up a handful of snow and threw it into the young man's face; he jumped aside and avoided being hit. She heard him laugh.

'I forbid you to touch me,' she shouted in a rage. 'Do you hear me?' And she ran along the dark frozen path in the direction of the house; she could feel the taste of eager young teeth on her lips, but she refused to allow her thoughts to linger there, to savour this new, passionate joy.

'Kissing me as if I were some chambermaid,' she thought, and she didn't stop running until she'd reached her mother's room. With only a cursory knock she burst in.

Bella and Max were sitting on the settee in silence. Hélène had seen, walked in on, many other couples. But what troubled her this time was something strange, something new, something tender about the intimacy of these two people, the aura of love that surrounded them, not vice or passion, but the most human, the most ordinary kind of love.

Bella slowly turned her head. 'What is it?'

'Nothing,' said Hélène, her heart aching, 'nothing . . . I thought . . . I . . .' She fell silent.

'Go outside, then,' said her mother. 'It isn't dark yet. I saw Fred Reuss; he was looking for you. Go out with him and the children . . .'

'Do you want me to go and find him?' asked Hélène, a melancholy, sarcastic little smile hovering on her lips. 'I'll go if you want me to . . .'

'Yes,' said Bella, 'off you go.'

# 4

The next day was a Sunday. Hélène walked into the little sitting room and breathed on the frozen windows to see the sky. Everything seemed extraordinarily joyous, clear and peaceful; children dressed in white played in the snow-covered garden; the sun was shining; the house smelled of warm cakes and cream, mixed with the scent of newly cleaned wooden floors. You could breathe in the day with all its freedom and innocence.

Hélène smiled as she stood in front of the old mirror; it reflected the sun as a distant, hazy, bluish form, like when you lean over water on a summer's day; she looked at her starched white linen dress; she saw Fred Reuss come in and, without turning round, nodded at him in the mirror.

They were alone. He pulled her against him less harshly than the day before, but with a kind of mocking tenderness that was unfamiliar to her. She let him kiss her, even leaned in towards him, offering her face, her hands, her lips, savouring waves of delight, aching waves of bliss that pierced straight through her body.

She felt he was younger than she was, with a persistent, eternal kind of youthfulness, which, in her eyes, was undoubtedly his most attractive feature. He was as tender, giving, trusting, mischievous, hot-blooded and happy as a child. When they played together in the snow with his two boys, she sensed that he didn't go endlessly up and down the little hill in order to be with them, nor even to be able secretly to kiss her, but rather because, like her, he loved more than anything the pure air, the sun, shouting and falling into the soft, damp snow. From that moment on they spent nearly all their time together. Hélène felt the most delicious, the most indulgent tenderness towards him, a tenderness that continued to grow, ever intensifying the exciting taste of his kisses. But what she liked most was the feeling of pride he gave her, her awareness of her power as a woman. She so enjoyed seeing Fred choose her over the young women who looked down on her because they were twenty! Sometimes she deliberately distanced herself from him, enjoying his silent fury when, instead of meeting him in the garden where he was waiting for her, she would go and sit beside his wife, eyes lowered, and sew. Then he would grab her by the hair as she ran down the stairs on to the terrace and whisper angrily, 'So young and already as horrible as a real woman!'

Then he would laugh, and Hélène never tired of seeing the little grimace at the corner of his mouth, the flash of desire that turned his face pale. Nevertheless, he knew what kind of power he held over her.

'When you're older, you'll think of me with gratitude, because if I'd wanted to . . . First of all, I could have made you suffer so much that it would haunt you for the rest of your life and you would never again have such absolute confidence about love. And also . . . you'll understand what I mean later on and you'll feel a great deal of friendship for me. You'll say: "He was a good-for-nothing, a womaniser, but with me he did the right thing." Either that, or: "What a fool he was." It will depend a lot on what kind of husband you end up with . . .'

It was nearly spring; the shiny tree trunks, damp and dark, seemed to be coming alive through some secret force. Beneath the thick layer of snow you could hear the first rush of trapped water breaking free; the ditches, no longer covered in fresh snow, were black with dried mud. Every day the sound of the cannons grew clearer: the White Army, the ordinary troops that would later become the army of the new republic, was making its way down from the north.

Everyone had lost their calm and arrogance: in their rooms at night they feverishly sewed shares and foreign money into their belts and the linings of their clothing. Amid this turmoil no one gave a thought to Hélène or Fred Reuss. They sat in the sitting room, where the windows glowed red as soon as night fell, for the fires were getting closer, a moving, pulsating circle that surrounded the village; and when the wind blew in from the east, it brought with it the faint smell of smoke and gunpowder. Hélène and Fred were alone; they exchanged long, silent kisses on the hard little bamboo settee that swayed and creaked in the darkness. The door was open and they could hear the sound of footsteps and voices in the hall. There was a shortage of oil, so the lamp gave off an intermittent reddish glow. Hélène forgot everything else in the world; she was sitting on Fred's lap; she could feel his heart beneath her cheek; it was pounding, missing a beat; she loved his dark, smiling eyes that closed so sensuously.

'Your wife . . . Be careful!' she would sometimes say, without moving.

But he didn't hear her; he was slowly drinking in the breath from her parted lips.

'Ah, leave me in peace, it's so dark, no one will see us. And besides, I don't care,' he murmured, 'I don't care about anything . . .'

'How quiet the house is tonight,' she said at last, pulling away from him.

He lit a cigarette and sat down on the window ledge. The night was impenetrable, heavy, without even a trace of light; ice in the shape of teardrops sparkled on the windows. The old pine trees gently creaked; their branches swished with a stifled sound, like someone sighing. Between the trees the light of a lantern suddenly appeared.

'What's that?' Hélène asked absent-mindedly.

Reuss didn't reply; leaning out of the window, he watched the lights as they moved, for there were many now; they had sprung up all over, flickering, disappearing, reappearing, criss-crossing like dancers in a ballet. He shrugged his shoulders. 'I don't understand . . . I can see one, two, three, women's cloaks,' he said, pressing his face to the window, 'but what can they be looking for here? They're looking for something in the snow,' he said again, counting each of the little flames that encircled the house, until gradually they disappeared.

He walked back over to Hélène, who sat motionless; she smiled, finding it hard to keep her eyes open: from dawn until dusk they'd played on sledges, skied, raced through the countryside, and these endless kisses . . . When night fell all she dreamed of was her bed and the long, wonderful hours of sleep until morning.

He sat down beside her and began kissing her again without worrying about the open door. Feeling eager excitement, she basked in these slow, silent kisses, in the reddish glow of the lamp that flickered and smoked, in this perfect security, this lightness, this feeling that the entire world could crumble around them and that nothing would ever be as wonderful as the taste of his moist mouth that she clung to with hers, the way he caressed her with his strong, supple hands. Sometimes she would stretch out her arms and push him away.

'What's the matter?' he would say. 'Am I frightening you?'

'No. Why?' she would reply. And her childlike innocence, as she allowed herself to be kissed like a woman, aroused his desire even more.

'Hélène,' he whispered.

'Yes?'

He murmured something; his words tailed away as if by some mysterious intoxication; his pale skin, his dishevelled hair, his trembling lips terrified her, but what she felt most was the sensation of wild, proud pleasure.

'Do you love me?'

'No,' she said, smiling.

He would never hear a word of affection from her, a confession of love.

'He doesn't love me,' she thought. 'He's getting pleasure out of this and it's only because I don't act like a docile, silly little girl in love that he still wants me and doesn't get bored with me.'

She thought she was so wise, so mature, so womanly . . .

'I don't love you, my darling, but I like you,' she said.

He pushed her away angrily. 'You little hag, get away, I hate you!'

Madame Haas came into the room. 'Have you seen what's going on?' she exclaimed, upset.

'No, what is it?'

She didn't reply, just picked up the lamp, held it up to the window and used the flames to melt the ice that covered the glass. 'I'm sure I saw the servants leave, an hour ago. They were running towards the forest and they haven't come back.'

She pressed her face against the window, but it was pitch dark outside; she opened the window a bit; her grey hair flew about in the wind.

'Where were they going? It's impossible to see anything. This will all end badly. The White Army is getting closer every day. Do you think they'll come and warn us when they intend to take over the village? But who listens to an old woman? You'll see, though, you'll see! I hope to God I'm wrong, but I can feel something bad is happening,' she cried, her voice shrill and plaintive, shaking her head like an elderly Cassandra.

Hélène stood up, walked over to the kitchen door and opened it; they saw that the fire was lit and continued to burn in the empty room, lighting up the table that had been laid with crockery and the food for dinner. But not a single soul was in the large room, normally full of the sound of voices and footsteps. The laundry room next door was also deserted, but the ironing boards had been left open with damp sheets carefully hanging over them: it looked as if someone had come to fetch the servants and they had immediately run away.

Hélène went outside and stood on the steps; she called out, but no one replied.

'They took the dogs!' she said, going back inside as she shook the snow from her bare head. 'I can't hear them, yet they know my voice very well . . .'

A woman appeared. 'The White Army is surrounding the village!' she shouted.

Doors opened; everyone held a lit candle, for it was the only way to light the house and these little flickering flames flew from room to room; the children woke up and started crying.

Hélène went back into the sitting room; it had gradually filled up with people. The women pressed their faces to the windows; they spoke to each other quietly.

'But it isn't possible . . . we would have heard them . . .'

'Why? Do you think they make announcements?' asked Madame Haas sarcastically.

'Get that woman out of here,' Reuss whispered in Hélène's ear. 'If I have to listen to her any more I'll wring the old crow's neck.'

'Listen!' cried Hélène.

The kitchen door banged violently in the silence. Everyone stopped talking.

One of the servants appeared at the door; she was an elderly Russian cook whose son was in the Red Guard; her cloak was covered in snow and her face looked exhausted and defeated; her dishevelled white hair fell over her forehead.

She looked at the women all around her, crossed herself and said, 'Pray for the souls of Hjalmar, Ivan, Olaf and Eric. They were taken prisoner tonight by the White Army, along with some other boys from the village. They were taken and shot, then their bodies were just thrown somewhere in the forest. We women went to look for the bodies to bury them, but the priest refused to let us into the cemetery, saying that Communist dogs didn't deserve any graves on Christian soil. We're going to bury them in the forest ourselves. God help us!'

She slowly walked away and closed the door. Hélène opened the window and watched them disappear into the night, each one carrying a shovel and a lantern that lit up the snow.

'But what about us? Us!' yelled Levy. 'What's going to happen to us in all this?'

Behind Hélène, a mass of buzzing voices rose up.

'We have nothing to fear from the White Army, that's for sure, but we've landed right in the middle of a battlefield. The best thing would be to leave right now.'

'Didn't I say that?' murmured the elderly Madame Haas with deep satisfaction.

'Fred,' asked Zenia Reuss, 'should we wake the children?'

'Of course. And be sure to dress them very warmly. Who wants to go with me to get the horses?'

'Wait until morning,' Madame Haas advised anxiously. 'It's too dark out. You might get caught in the crossfire. And besides, where would you go in the middle of the night, in this cold, with women and children?'

All the mothers had appeared by now, each holding a child in her arms. They weren't crying but stared in wide-eyed surprise. Reuss suggested they play cards to make the time pass more quickly, so they set up the bridge tables as they did every night. Hélène looked around her; all the children, big or little, were sitting next to their mothers, and each mother had placed a trembling hand on their bent shoulders and foreheads, as if their delicate hands had the power to stop bullets.

Reuss went over to his wife and tenderly placed his hand on her arm. 'Don't be afraid, my darling, you mustn't be afraid, we're together,' he whispered, and Hélène felt an invisible vice tightening round her heart.

'He loves her so very much . . . But of course he loves her: she's his wife,' she thought with stifled anger. 'What's got into me? But all the same, I'm so very alone . . .'

She walked away, sat down on the window ledge and absent-mindedly watched the snow as it fell.

'The way he looks at her!' she thought, tortured by a kind of suffering she'd never felt before. 'The way he takes his sons' hands! He loves his children so much. Oh, look how much he cares about me now, me whom he kissed and caressed so tenderly just five minutes ago. I'm so glad I didn't say "I love you". But do I love him? I don't know. I'm in pain, it's not fair, I wasn't meant to suffer like this, I'm too young . . .'

She looked at her mother and Max with hatred.

'It's because of them . . .' She turned towards Max. 'I hate him, I could kill him,' she thought, but then, as the pathetic childish curses rose to her lips, she had an idea.

'How stupid I am! Vengeance is within my grasp. I knew how to get Fred Reuss when all the women were after him. Max is just a man. If I wanted to . . . Oh, my God, don't tempt me. But . . . she deserves it. My poor Mademoiselle Rose. How they made her suffer. Forgive them? Why? Why should I? Yes, I know. God said: "Vengeance is mine . . ." Well, too bad. I'm not a saint; I can't forgive her. Wait, just you wait and you'll see. I'll make you cry the way you made me cry. You never taught me goodness, forgiveness. It's very simple: you never taught me anything but to be afraid of you and how to behave at mealtimes. Everything is hateful, I'm suffering, the world is evil. Wait, just you wait, you old . . . !'

The lamp flickered one last time and went out. The men swore and waved their lit cigarettes about.

'Well! There's not a drop of petrol, of course, and there's no one in the kitchen . . .'

'I know where the candles are,' said Hélène.

She found two candles; one was placed among the men playing cards and the other on the piano, the only light in the shabby little room that Hélène was never to see again.

The children fell asleep. Every now and again one of the men said, 'Really, we'd be better off going to bed to get some rest. It's ridiculous sitting here. What good are we doing?'

But the women said over and over again, nervously, 'Let's stay together, we feel better when we're all together . . .'

It was nearly midnight when they heard the first gunshots. The men turned white and dropped their cards. Sometimes the shooting came closer, then sounded far away.

'Put out the lights,' someone cried anxiously.

They rushed to the candles and blew them out. In the darkness, Hélène could hear the sound of panicked breathlessness and murmurs of 'My God, my God, dear Lord God . . .'

Hélène laughed to herself; she liked the sound of the gunfire; a wild exhilaration made her shudder and quiver with joy.

'They're so afraid. They're so upset, all of them! *I'm* not afraid. *I* won't let anyone frighten me. I'm enjoying myself, I'm enjoying this,' she mused; and to her the battle, the danger, the risk were all transformed into a terrible but exciting game; she suddenly felt herself stronger, more mockingly detached than she had ever felt before or would ever feel again. She was eager to enjoy the feeling, as if she had a premonition that from this moment on, everyone she loved in the future, every child she might love, would steal a little bit of this strength, this cold-blooded courage from her, leaving her just like everyone else, part of the herd, pressing their families, their own flesh and blood, tightly against them in the darkness. No one spoke. Every mother covered her children with her skirts to protect them from the cold night, all the while convinced that none of them would live to see the dawn. She could hear belts full of gold creaking in the darkness; a child was crying softly. Old Haas's shawl slipped to the ground; he moaned and sighed pleadingly; his elderly wife worried that anxiety and the freezing cold night would kill him: he had a heart condition. Tears of irritation fell down her face.

'My God! You can be such a nuisance,' she said, sounding angry yet loving, 'My poor husband . . .'

Max and Fred Reuss had gone to the village to try to find some horses. The night passed by. They still hadn't returned.

'Does anyone have any spirits?' asked Madame Reuss. 'We must give them something to drink when they get back. It's such a cold night.'

She spoke in a soft, calm voice, as if she were talking about a peaceful stroll on the plains.

Hélène shrugged her shoulders. 'Poor woman,' she thought. 'Doesn't she realise they might never make it back?'

Madame Haas went into her room, clattering the keys that swung from her belt; she soon returned with a flask of alcohol. Madame Reuss took the bottle and thanked her. It was only when someone used his cigarette lighter that Hélène could see how deathly pale the young woman's face was.

'She loves him too much to give up hope,' she thought, as regret – regret she felt too late – rose up in her soul. 'When you love someone as much as that, you don't believe they can die. You think your love protects them. Even if he doesn't come back, even if he gets lost in the snow or is hit by a stray bullet, she'll wait for him . . . faithfully. Is it possible she hasn't noticed anything? Oh, quite the opposite, she has known for a long time, but she must be used to it. She says nothing. She's right. Her Fred really does belong to her.'

She looked at her mother, who was trembling and anxiously trying to find a light in the dark night.

'But why are you so anxious, my dear?' Madame Haas said to her. 'Your daughter is with you.' Her voice was soft and malicious.

It seemed to Hélène that all the people gathered there were opening up their hearts to her, without intending to; she was sitting on the window ledge, swinging her legs towards the shapeless mass huddled in the darkness, listening to the sound of incessant gunfire; it was low-pitched and intense. A few minutes later they all left the room and climbed up the stairs, for they were afraid that stray bullets might come in through the windows. Hélène alone remained there with the young woman with tuberculosis; she had silently come in, sat down on the piano stool and started to play, feeling her way across the keyboard, separating herself from the families who were as warm and loving as cattle in a stable. Hélène pulled back a shutter; at once the moonlight shimmered on to the keyboard and the thin hands that played such passionate, impish music.

'Mozart,' said the young woman.

Then they fell silent. They had never exchanged a single word; they would never see each other again. Hélène held her head in her hands and listened to the tender, delicate, mocking harmonies, the clear, light chords, the laughter that scoffed at darkness and death, and she felt the dizzying, proud exhilaration of being herself, Hélène Karol, 'stronger, freer than all of them . . .'.

In the morning someone called her: the horses were there.

'There might not be enough room for everyone,' said Reuss. 'Women and children first.'

But everyone said, 'No. We all go together.'

Bella took Max's hand. 'All together . . .'

Only then did she remember that Hélène was there. 'Do you have your coat? And a shawl?' she asked quickly. 'I still have to think of everything for a girl your age.'

Hélène made her way over to Reuss. 'Where are you going? Can't we go together?'

'No. We have to go our separate ways at the edge of the forest so we don't attract attention, and everyone will go with his own family.'

'I understand,' she murmured.

Their carriages were waiting, lined up outside the door, just as when they were going to dance with the Red Guard, all now dead and buried.

The horizon was lit up with distant fires, and the pine trees covered in snow looked pink beneath the soft grey sky of the early dawn.

'This is goodbye,' said Fred. He secretly pressed his lips against Hélène's cold cheek.

'Goodbye,' he said softly, 'my poor darling . . .'

They walked away from each other.

# 5

After a long, exhausting journey the Karols ended up in Helsinki in the spring; it was a bright, peaceful, happy little town. Lilac bushes were in blossom in every street. It was the time of year when the sky is never dark, but keeps a milky light until morning, like the soft transparency of dusk in May.

Hélène was sent to board with Fru Martens, the widow of a Finnish minister, a respectable person with many virtues and many children. She was a short, thin, supple woman with blond hair, dry skin and a pinkish nose that had been frozen some time in the past and was now chapped and purplish in the middle. She taught Hélène German and read her *Mutter Sorge* out loud. While she read, Hélène watched a little pointy bone move around beneath the yellowish skin of her old neck, as prominent as an Adam's apple; she didn't listen to a word, daydreaming instead.

She wasn't unhappy, just bored to tears. It wasn't only Fred Reuss she missed. Quite the opposite, she had forgotten Fred Reuss strangely quickly. But she missed the freedom, the open spaces, the danger, the full life she had led that she couldn't erase from her memory.

In the evening, when the little Martenses sang '*Tannenbaum, oh, Tannenbaum, wie grün sind deine Blätter!*' she listened with pleasure to their soft, sonorous voices, but at the same time she would think, 'Oh, for the sound of cannons! For danger, anything just to feel alive! To live! Or to be a child like the others . . . But no, it's too late for that. I'm only sixteen, but my heart is filled with poison.'

The autumn moon spread its cool, clear light over the little sitting room and its ornamental green pot plants; she walked over to the window and looked at the bay shimmering in the darkness.

'I want my revenge. Will I have to die without ever getting back at them?'

Ever since the night when the idea first crossed her mind she continually embellished it, enjoyed it.

'To take her Max away from her! To make both of them suffer the way they made me suffer! I didn't ask to be born. Oh, how I would have preferred never to have been born. No one gave a thought to me, that's for sure. They brought me into this world and left me to grow up alone. Well, that's not enough! It's a crime to have children and not give them an atom, a crumb of love. I can't give up the idea of revenge. Don't make me, Lord! I think I would rather die than give up that idea. To take her lover away from her! Me, little Hélène!'

Only on Sundays did Hélène see her mother and Max. They would arrive together, stay a short time, then leave. Sometimes Max would place a few marks on the table: 'You can buy yourself some sweets . . .'

After he left she would give the money to the servants and it would take a very long time to stop her entire body from quivering with hatred.

In the meantime she noticed that something had changed between her mother and Max: it was a subtle change and difficult to define. But the way they spoke to one another was different and so were their silences. They had always quarrelled, but now the tone of their arguments was more bitter, full of impatience and anger.

'They're becoming a married couple!' Hélène mused.

She cruelly studied her mother's face for a long time; she could watch her as much as she liked: her mother's harsh eyes never fell on her; Bella seemed completely transfixed by Max; she would eagerly scrutinise every change in his features, while he looked away, as if he could barely stand her looking at him.

Bella's face was beginning to age; its muscles were slackening; Hélène could see wrinkles beneath the powder and rouge that the make-up filled in without being able to hide; they stood out as deep, fine lines at the corners of her eyes, her lips and on her temples. The painted surface of her skin was cracking, losing its smooth, creamy texture, becoming coarser, rougher. On her neck appeared the triple creases that meant she was in her forties.

One day they arrived after a longer, more serious quarrel than usual: Hélène could tell immediately by the sad, annoyed expression on her mother's face, by the quivering of her tense mouth.

Bella angrily took off her fur coat and threw it on to the bed. 'It's so hot in here. Are you working hard, Hélène? You did nothing all last year. Look at what a mess your hair is. You look five years older than you are with your hair pulled back like that, I have no desire to be burdened with a daughter to marry off. Oh, Max, stop turning round in circles like a caged animal! Hélène, ask them to bring us some tea.'

'At this hour?'

'Well, what time is it, then?'

'Seven o'clock. I was expecting you earlier.'

'You can surely wait an hour for your mother. Ah, how ungrateful children are. Just like everyone else in the world. There's not a single soul who loves you, who feels sorry for you! Not one . . .'

'Are you really someone we should feel sorry for?' Hélène asked softly.

'I'm dying of thirst,' said Bella. She got a glass of water and drank it quickly. Her eyes were full of tears. When she put down the glass, Hélène saw her secretly shape her eyebrows with her finger and look anxiously at her face in the mirror: the tears were damaging her make-up.

'This is becoming unbearable!' Max muttered through tight lips.

'Oh, really, is that what you think? And what about the night I spent waiting for you, while your friends and those women . . .'

'What women?' he said with a weary sigh. 'You'd like to lock me behind closed doors so that I see, hear and live for nothing but you.'

'Before . . .'

'Yes, exactly, that was before! How can you not understand? We're only young once, only free once. It might be all right to throw everything out of the window, your

family, your past, your future, once . . . at twenty-four. But
life goes on, people change, become more serious, wiser.
Whereas you . . . you . . . You're tyrannical, egotistical,
demanding. You make yourself unbearable to others and
to yourself. I've been unhappy recently, you can see that
very well. I'm sad, tired of it all, irritable. You take no pity
on me. Yet all I ask of you is one thing. Leave me alone!
Don't have me trailing behind you like a dog on a leash.
Let me breathe!'

'But what on earth is wrong with you? Imagine, Hélène.
He hasn't had any letters from his mother, no letters from
his beloved mother. But is that my fault? I'm asking you, is
that my fault?'

Max struck his fist angrily against the table. 'Is this any
business of the child's? Oh, enough, enough of your
tears! I swear to you, Bella, if you start crying again I'm
going to leave and you'll never see me again as long as I
live. At least, in the past, you were as hard on yourself as
you were on everyone else. That was rather attractive,' he
said more quietly. 'In my heart I called you Medea. But
now . . .'

'Yes,' mused Hélène, silent and invisible in the dark
room, 'you're getting old. Every day that passes robs you
of a weapon and adds one to my armoury. I'm young; I'm
only sixteen, I'll steal your lover from you and, sadly, it
won't take very long or need much cunning. It won't be
very difficult. And when I've made you really suffer, I'll
send him packing, because, to me, he'll always be the Max
I hated from my childhood, the enemy of that poor dead
woman. Oh, how I will avenge her. But I still need to wait
a while longer . . .'

She had vague memories of those childhood evenings: coming home from the park, dying of thirst as she walked beneath the shady lime trees, breathing in their perfume and dreaming of the cold milk that was waiting for her in a blue bowl; she remembered how she would half close her eyes to quench the thirst within her by imagining the sweet, cool liquid and the feeling of ice-cold milk flowing down her throat; how, once inside her room, she would hold the bowl in her hands for a long time, then bring it close to her face and moisten her lips with the milk before greedily drinking it down.

Suddenly the telephone rang. Hélène picked up the receiver; someone wanted to speak to Max. 'It's for you, Max,' she said. 'Some news from Constantinople. They're calling from your house.'

Max grabbed the phone from her. She saw his face contort with pain. He listened for a moment without saying a word, then hung up and turned towards Bella. 'Well,' he said quietly, 'you can be happy now. I'm all yours. I have nothing left, nothing apart from you. My mother has died. All alone, just as she predicted. Oh, I'll be punished, terribly punished! That's what it was, then, this weight that was suffocating me. She died in the hospital in Constantinople; strangers had to tell me she'd died. She was alone. But what about my sisters? What happened to them during that journey when I wasn't at their side to protect them, to help them, while I was with you, with you and your family? I'll never forgive you for this!'

'But you're mad!' cried Bella in tears, leaning towards him, her face distorted as her make-up ran. 'Is this my fault? Don't be so cruel. Don't push me away! You're punishing me for your own mistakes. Is that fair? Yes, I wanted you to stay, to keep you with me. What woman would have done anything different? Is it my fault?'

'Everything is your fault!' he shouted, angrily pushing her away.

She clung on to his clothes.

'Oh, enough, enough!' he said with hatred. 'We're not in the fifth act of some melodrama. Let go of me.'

He opened the door.

'You won't leave me!' Bella cried. 'You have no right to leave me. Forgive me, Max, forgive me. Listen, I'm stronger than you think. I have more power over you than you know! You couldn't leave me . . .'

Hélène heard the door slam in the empty street. 'Be quiet,' she said, shaking with anger. 'I'm begging you. We're not in our own house.'

Bella wrung her hands in distress. 'And that's all you have to say to me? You can see how terribly upset I am. You have no pity. Won't you even come and give me a kiss? Didn't you see how he treats me? His mother died of breast cancer. Is that my fault?'

'It's nothing to do with me,' said Hélène.

'You're sixteen. You understand life. You understand very well.'

'I don't want to understand . . .'

'You miserable little egotist; you're heartless. You're my daughter, after all! Not a word of affection . . . Not even a kiss!'

Fru Martens put her head round the door. 'Dinner is served. Come and sit down, Helenchen.'

Hélène leaned towards her mother for a kiss, but she turned

away; Hélène went and sat down with Fru Martens, who was already standing in front of the steaming soup tureen saying grace. Hélène's heart was pounding with hatred and anger. 'Oh,' she mused, 'it really would be too easy!'

# PART IV

# 1

The winds of war, which scattered men all over the world, carried the Karols to France in July 1919.

A few months before, Boris Karol had crossed Finland, lost five million Swedish crowns on the exchange rate, got two million back and left again for Paris, where his wife, his daughter and Max were to join him.

The ship approached the English coast the day after the Treaty of Versailles had been signed. It was as cold and foggy as an autumn night; the bright stars peeked out or appeared briefly from behind the clouds, only to be hidden again. There were lights everywhere: strings of paper lanterns linked the little coastal towns to form a single chain of flickering yellow light surrounded by a halo that shimmered gently through the damp sea fog. Fireworks shot into the sky, some exploding, others leaving only a coppery trail of smoke behind them. The wind carried snatches of military music towards the ship, but those heroic fanfares were unable to dispel the solemn melancholy of the long night: the exhilaration of the Armistice was long gone, leaving behind only a heavy, awkward attempt at joy.

An English pilot came on board; he was so drunk he could hardly walk. He had a Cockney accent. '*Every man on land is married tonight, Ladies . . .*' he sang in a thick voice full of emotion.

To get away from him, Hélène went and hid in her favourite place, at the front of the ship, where the captain's tan bulldog chewed quietly at the rigging. For a long time, she looked at the coast of France that bobbed gently up and down before her in the night. She looked at it with tenderness. Her heart had never beaten as joyously when she'd gone back to Russia. The coast of France seemed to be welcoming her, celebrating her arrival, with lights and fireworks flying high above the sea. The closer she got, the more she felt she recognised the smell of the wind; she closed her eyes. It had been five years since she'd seen that sweet land, the most beautiful place in the world. That brief length of time seemed like an eternity to her: she had seen so many things; she had changed from a child into a young woman. A world had crumbled, dragging innumerable men to their death, but she didn't think about that, or rather a kind of fierce egotism kept watch within her to prevent her from thinking about it. With the merciless harshness of youth she rejected any morbid memories; she retained only an awareness of her strength, her age, her intoxicating power. Little by little, a feeling of primitive exhilaration filled her being. She jumped on to the pile of ropes better to breathe in the wind. The sea shimmered slightly, illuminated by the lights on the ship. She felt almost weightless, as if lifted into the air with joy, carried away by a force more powerful than herself. 'This is youth,' she mused, smiling. 'There's no better feeling in the world.'

She saw Max coming towards her; she recognised his walk and the glow of the little pipe he was smoking. 'Is that you?' he asked wearily.

He went over to her, leaned against the railings next to her and watched the sea in silence; one of the ship's lanterns lit up his face. How he had changed! He was one of those men who, when they are young, seem to have finer features and look more handsome than they actually are; he wasn't even thirty, but already his clean-shaven face, drawn at the corners of his mouth, was thicker, heavier; it had begun to crumple, turn ugly; he no longer had his beautiful silky eyelashes or the scornful crease at the corner of his handsome mouth; it was paler now, leaving him looking weary and irritated; you could see the gold fillings in his teeth.

He whistled softly to the dog. 'Up, Svea, you're in my spot. Move over a bit, Hélène.'

He came and sat down beside her, holding the bulldog on his lap.

'Those lights to the right,' said Hélène softly, 'that must be Le Havre. How bright it looks. I think I can make out the coastline near Honfleur. Yes, it's France, France!'

'You're happy, aren't you?' he asked, sighing.

'Yes. Why wouldn't I be? I love France, and those lights are a good omen.'

'Presumptuous youth,' he scoffed. 'The lights, the music, the shouting . . . You don't see them as being in honour of an event as insignificant as the signing of a peace treaty. In your eyes they're for you. How silly young girls can be.'

'Now, now,' she said, taking his hand. 'You'd be quite happy to be in my shoes. Look at you. Fed up, irritable . . . and why? *I'm* content, I feel light-hearted, happy. And it's because I'm seventeen, darling, and that's a joyful time of life.'

She slowly raised her bare arm to her lips and licked the smooth, suntanned skin to taste the salt left there by ten days at sea.

Max looked at her with curiosity. 'Shall I tell you something?' he asked after thinking for a moment. 'I hope you won't be offended. You haven't grown up in the way you'd like me to think, you've simply got younger. At fifteen you were a little old lady. Now, at last, you're the age you should be.'

'Well, well,' she whispered, 'so you've noticed that?'

He nodded. 'I notice everything, understand everything, and when I don't understand, it's because I don't want to.'

'Oh, really?' she said, while she was actually thinking, 'So, the game is on. We'll soon see who wins . . .'

She was trembling with a cunning, cruel excitement, but at the same time she felt truly sad. 'I'm no better than them, in the end . . .'

She remembered an unhappy little girl whose heart was filled with love; she affectionately contemplated that image, deep within her, and spoke to it: 'Patience, you'll see . . .'

The ship sailed on between the two illuminated coastlines; between France and England, fanfare answered fanfare as fireworks mirrored fireworks; and in the reddish sea mist the boat slowly drifted towards the brightly shining ports decorated with flags and banners.

Hélène clenched her trembling hands together in a child-like gesture, just as she had in the past. 'I used to come here when I was a child. It was the only place in the world that

I was happy,' she said softly, expecting him to respond with the dry little scornful laugh she knew so well.

But at first he didn't reply at all and, when he did speak, his voice was different: gentle and hesitant. 'I know you didn't have a happy childhood. You see, Hélène, sometimes people are bad without realising it. You can't always make your life turn out the way you want it to be. You're at an age when . . .'

He fell silent.

'I wonder if you would understand the real meaning of the word passion?'

He smoked for a moment in silence, looking up at the stars. 'They're barely shining . . . The lights from the ground are masking them . . . What was I saying? Yes, passion . . . Take your father, for example. He's passionate about gambling and it's an invincible, horrible obsession. You belong to a race of passionate people, my poor Hélène, who abandon themselves to their obsessions completely, ignoring any sense of duty or morality. That's just how they are. You won't change them. *I'm* not like them. It's just that there are certain ties that can't be undone, ties that keep you tightly bound, that strangle you. I know I can behave badly, but at least I feel regret, I can't forget everything else in the world. I don't understand that obsession, that cruelty. I thought I did understand . . .'

He turned away and slowly placed his hand over his eyes, feeling ashamed and almost certainly wiping away a tear. 'I don't know what's come over me,' he said at last. 'Since my mother died, Hélène, I feel so depressed. Oh, it's so sad, you have no idea. I loved my mother so much . . . To other people she seemed harsh and cold. But when it came to me, she loved me so much. Whenever I walked over to her I could see her face change, light up, not with a smile, but with a kind of inner light, a light that shone only for me.'

At first she listened to him with astonishment. To her, the love of a child for a mother was not a feeling easy to understand. But then she started to think he was wallowing in his sorrow, feeding it with all the anger he felt towards Bella and her tyrannical, all-consuming love.

Meanwhile, he was remembering something his mother had said to him one day when they were quarrelling a very long time ago. It made him feel uneasy: 'And one fine day you'll marry Hélène. That's what always happens in the end.' He had laughed at the time. Now he smiled, for when someone is dead, certain insignificant words they've said take on a new, prophetic, threatening meaning. He pushed the memory from his thoughts.

'If you like,' Hélène said softly, 'we could be . . . good friends . . .'

He sighed. 'I'd like that very much. I hardly have any friends. I have no friends at all.' He squeezed her hand. 'You know, we could have been friends a long time ago, if you'd wanted to. But you were horrible . . .'

'Now, now,' she said, laughing, 'don't push it. We've also signed a peace treaty tonight, you and I . . .' She jumped down. 'I'm going to bed.'

'Where's your mother?'

'Asleep. She can't stand it when the ship rocks.'

'Ah,' he murmured, his thoughts elsewhere. 'Goodnight . . .'

Oddly enough, the cargo boat was transporting a shipment of theatre sets from Norkøping to Le Havre. The sea was so choppy that they couldn't anchor in Le Havre, so the ship followed the estuary of the Seine to Rouen. In the morning the countryside was full of fruit trees. Hélène stood dead still, rooted to the spot with surprise, looking at the peaceful landscape. Apple trees . . . It seemed as extraordinary to her as seeing palm trees, or bread and cheese hanging from the branches. Then Rouen appeared and, that very evening, they were in Paris.

In Paris, Karol was waiting for them. He was thinner; his clothing hung off his hunched shoulders in great folds; beneath the thin, dry skin on his face the outline of his bones appeared so distinctly that you could follow the line of his strong jaw; his eyes had blackish-brown circles round them; every one of his gestures was nervous and hesitant; he seemed consumed from within by some inner fire.

He briefly kissed his daughter, slapped Max on the back, then turned round and affectionately took Bella's arm and held her close. 'Ah, my darling, my darling wife . . .'

Then, immediately, a flood of incomprehensible words and numbers washed over Hélène's head.

Paris was sad, deserted, lit up only by the odd street lamp and the bright stars. Hélène recognised each of the streets.

They crossed the Place Vendôme; it was dark and empty.

Bella pouted and said, 'So this is Paris? My God, how it's changed!'

'We're making money everywhere we turn,' whispered Karol. 'We rolling in it.'

# 2

That autumn, Karol left for New York, leaving his wife a new car whose wheels and headlights sparkled with gold.

Sometimes the chambermaid would wake Hélène early in the morning with news that they were leaving in an hour. Where were they going? No one knew. The morning would pass. The car would wait. The servants would carry down Bella's cases, hatboxes and toiletries. Then the chambermaid would cross the entrance hall carrying the jewellery box and make-up case, sit down in the back of the car and wait. Max and Bella were quarrelling. Hélène could hear them from her room, first cold and calm, then gradually becoming more and more passionate and full of hate.

'Never again, I swear it!'

'Stop making a scene . . .'

'A scene! You poison the existence of everyone around you . . .'

'In the past . . .'

'In the past, I was mad. When a madman recovers his sanity, should he remain locked up in his cell for ever?'

'Well, then, get out, who's stopping you?'

'If you say that one more time . . .'

'Why not? Go on, that's right, get out, you miserable, ungrateful thing. No, no, Max, my darling, forgive me, forgive me. Don't look at me like that . . .'

By now it was nearly twelve o'clock. They had to have lunch. They ate in deadly silence. Bella, her eyes swollen from crying, stared out into the street. Max, his hands shaking, leafed through a Michelin guide whose pages tore when he touched them. The chambermaid had gone back upstairs to her room with the jewellery box and make-up case. The car sat waiting. The driver had fallen asleep at the wheel. A series of servants took the suitcases back upstairs.

Hélène went and knocked on her mother's door. 'Are we going somewhere today, Mama?'

'I don't know. Leave me alone. In any case, where could we go? It's late. Hélène, where are you, Hélène? Yes, we're leaving, right away, in an hour. But just go away. Leave me in peace, for the love of God! All of you, just leave me alone! You all wish I were dead!'

She was crying. The car still waited. Bella had the servant unpack her cosmetics and plastered make-up on again to repair her face.

'Do you know where we're going, Mademoiselle?' the driver asked.

Hélène didn't know. She waited. When her mother and Max finally came downstairs, pale and still shaking with fury, it was late. A delicate mist rose from the damp streets towards the clear red sky. They set off, randomly choosing one of the roads that led out of Paris. No one spoke. Bella's eyes filled with tears; she didn't wipe them away because she

didn't want to ruin her make-up, just dabbed at them nervously, recalling with pity and tenderness the woman she
used to be. Who in the world, apart from Karol perhaps,
remembered that young woman walking along the streets of
Paris one autumn evening, dressed in the latest 1905 fashion,
a large straw hat perched on top of her black chignon, its
short veil forming a tulle frame round her face? She was
young, then, rather awkward with too much perfume and
inexpensive make-up inexpertly applied, but her skin was so
white and smooth. Everything seemed wonderful to her.
Why did she get married? Why do people realise the existence that might have been theirs so late in life? Why did she
resist that Argentinean she'd known as a young woman? He
would have ended up leaving her, but there would have been
others to replace him. She wasn't a hypocrite. 'What do men
want from me?' she thought. 'I can't change my body or put
out the fire that burns in my blood. Was I made to be a good
wife and mother? Max fell in love with me because I was
nothing like those gloomy middle-class women he met, and
now he won't forgive me for having remained who I am. Is
that my fault?'

She remembered the Paris of her past, the day she had
first arrived there fifteen years before: the fine rain with its
smell of musk that fell slowly against a background of light.
Every house was lit up in the darkness. A man followed her.
He'd wanted her to go with him. Oh, how passionately she
had wished never again to return to Russia, never again to
see her husband and daughter, just to go away with him, not
because she loved him, but because he symbolised a free and
happy life. Happy? And why not? But she was still young
then and hadn't dared. She'd been afraid of having an affair

and being poor. She had still carried pictures of Boris and Hélène in a little silk bag sewn into her blouse, along with her passport and return ticket. Stupid, cowardly youth. Unique, irreplaceable youth! She felt as if Max had stolen it from her. Because of him, she had carelessly let time slip by, without thinking of holding on to those precious moments, without savouring each and every drop of happiness. And now, he didn't love her any more . . .

She turned towards him and looked at him through her tears. They had left Paris. They were driving through the countryside. Night had fallen. The scent of fresh grass rose from the meadows mingled with the smell of milk from the farms. They went past sleepy villages and, in the headlights of the car, they saw a white façade, a flashing traffic marker and, at the entrance to a church, white angels carved in stone, smiling mysteriously, their wings folded. A pale yellow dog or cat came out of the shadows, its flashing eyes reflecting the car's headlights, then an old woman appeared in a white dressing gown standing near the open shutters. The driver, who could barely keep his eyes open, grumbled, and the brakes screeched as he nervously applied them, but they kept going, like madmen, towards Normandy or Provence, while Bella said over and over again, 'We should have gone somewhere else. I don't like this road, I don't like this car. I'm bored with it all, everything is frustrating, sad, horrible.'

And her eyes fell upon the cold, motionless face beside her with love, despair and anguish.

At midnight, they stopped for dinner at an empty inn.

They ate, and Hélène waited for the quarrel to begin with malicious joy: always present, yet invisible, it seemed to simmer near the surface, like flames beneath the ashes.

'You really must have lost your mind to want to travel like this.'

'You could have stayed in Paris.'

'I swear that this is the last time I'll ever go with you.'

'You're such a bore.'

'And you are unbelievably selfish. You're on a diet, and you don't give a damn if everyone else is dying of hunger.'

'Please do not be crude in front of my daughter.'

'I'm not crude, but you are certainly mad.'

Hélène watched them, smiling. She deliberately reminded herself of the past, still so near, when she had sat between them this way and watched their every movement in terror, jumping every time they raised their voices, knowing very well that her mother's anger would inevitably fall back on to her because she was so weak, or on to Mademoiselle Rose. But now, nothing in the world had the power to make her suffer.

She ate, eagerly wolfing down the omelette cooked in lard and the cold meat; she drank the good wine and listened, with joyous scorn, to the quarrel that echoed in her ears, without being affected by it; it had lost its malevolent power, just as the sound of thunder in the theatre eventually ceases to frighten children. They hurled the simplest words at each other as if each one were a hammer; they repeated what they said, looked for the most insignificant words and found some hidden, obscure meaning in them; they recalled things that had happened a year ago, five years ago; pitilessly, they searched for words that could best be misinterpreted.

'People who love each other,' thought Hélène contemptuously.

But she was still too young to perceive the dying, bleeding love that remained between Max and his mistress of so long.

'How did this happen? And so quickly. He loved her so much,' she wondered. 'It must have happened in Finland, when I was in love with Fred, so I didn't notice . . .'

She studied them with sardonic pity as Bella pushed away her plate and started sobbing; her tears flowed down her face, ruining her make-up; in the past her tears would have pierced Max's heart, causing him a fierce, insidious pain. But now he simply clenched his teeth, anxiously looking around in anger.

'That's enough! You're embarrassing me,' he muttered, barely able to speak. He violently pushed back his chair. 'I've really had enough. If you want to come, then come. Let's go, Hélène.'

Bella powdered her face, still crying, her half-eaten food in front of her, and counted each new wrinkle that appeared beneath her tears with bitter despair; Max and Hélène stood on the doorstep, in the moonlight, and waited for her.

'Oh, Hélène,' he said in a weary, hoarse voice, 'my little Hélène, I'm so unhappy . . .'

'Don't exaggerate.'

'Well,' he replied angrily, 'that's very nice of you! You're not the one who's suffering.'

'No, that's true, I'm not suffering, not any more . . .'

Bella came and joined them and they left, driving through the night in silence.

The next day they arrived at one of the 'hostelries' that had started to spring up in the French countryside, where waitresses dressed in Normandy lace headdresses and pink taffeta aprons, as if they were in an operetta. They tottered across the lawns in their pointy high-heeled shoes, carrying fine wines in rustic jugs and, on a chipped earthenware plate decorated with flowers, a lunch bill for three or five or six hundred francs nonchalantly folded in half. This was inflation, fleeting prosperity. Long strands of pearls fell like serpents into the stinging nettles, and gigolos sprawled in the grass, third-rate 'darlings' with the hairy chests and damp hands of butcher boys.

It was only when evening fell and the couples disappeared that the scent of perfume and face powder began to fade; then you could smell the cold, damp, bitter Normandy forests. Max and Hélène spoke quietly together, while Bella, hidden by the darkness, tried out some new technique to tighten the muscles in her face. She would slowly lower her jaw twelve or fifteen times in a row, then tightly clench her teeth and pinch her mouth closed until the skin on her cheeks was taut to the point of tearing. She would tilt her head backwards, take a deep breath, then exhale slowly. She couldn't hear what Max and her daughter were saying. Hélène was still a child . . .

'Barely eighteen, a kid, he doesn't even look at her . . . But he misses the illusion of a family. At least, that's what he thinks. The child amuses him . . .' she thought.

Max and Hélène were talking about the little town on the Dnieper where they had spent their childhood. Memory had given it a melancholy charm. They happily thought back to the clear, icy air in autumn, the sleepy streets, the cooing of the woodpigeons, the Tsar's Park, the small green islands and golden church towers on the river.

'I remember your mother,' Hélène said. 'I remember the carriage and the horses. They were so fat! I wondered how they could move at all. Where did you live?'

'Oh, in a very, very ancient, wonderful house, where the parquet floors would creak beneath your feet because they were so old, I believe I can still remember the sound the floorboards made when you stepped on them. What I would give to have it all back!'

'How middle class,' said Bella with scorn. 'How very middle class. *I'm* happy here . . .'

She reached out her hand and took his in hers, squeezing it with desperate affection. 'With you,' she whispered.

He moved his chair away and gestured that Hélène was there; he looked upset and confused.

Hélène smiled sadly and thought, 'Too late, my darling . . .'

# 3

By the autumn the Karols no longer lived in a hotel; they
had a furnished apartment on the rue de la Pompe that had
previously belonged to an American woman who had married
an Italian duke. Every armchair was upholstered in velvet
embossed with family crests; the back of every chair was
topped with a crown sculpted in gilded wood. Boris Karol
sometimes absent-mindedly pulled off some pearls from the
crowns and rolled them around in his hand. Ever since he
had returned from America, a vague attempt at a family life
sometimes meant that Hélène, her parents and Max found
themselves all together. Karol leaned his head against the
cushion embroidered with some indefinable coat of arms,
looked at this wife and daughter and smiled. Such moments
were a respite in his life, a kind of sweet, ordinary pleasure
that he rarely enjoyed, and even then only for a short while,
but which brought him contentment, like drinking eggnog
when your stomach is sensitive from too much wine and
spicy food. Hélène recognised the expression she so rarely
saw on his face; she thought of it as 'Peace on earth good

will towards men'. Bella seemed more serious, calmer; these were moments when the fire that burned endlessly in her body died away. Max would smoke; Hélène would read; the lamplight would shine on Hélène's hair and Bella would say quietly, either to please her husband or because she wasn't entirely devoid of maternal instinct, despite it being dim and feeble, 'Hélène's starting to become a woman.'

She didn't notice how Max looked intensely at Hélène's bent head, then quickly turned away. But the more mellow her mother became, the more Hélène felt hatred stir in her heart, hatred that was even fiercer and more passionate than when she was a child.

'It would have taken so little back then,' she mused. 'Now it's too late. I'll never forgive her, never. I could forgive her if she hurt me now, the person I am now. Yes, I think I would forgive her. But you can't forgive someone for ruining your childhood.'

Sometimes she would raise her eyes and look deep into the mirror, searching for the round, tanned face she'd had as a child, for her wide mouth, her black curls. But all she saw was a young girl who was starting to become a woman, as Bella put it; she was losing her air of pride and innocence, and her cheekbones were beginning to stand out in her face, in the very place where, in years to come, the first wrinkles would appear . . .

Such were the family evenings spent in Paris, in this bustling and cold foreign city, in this furnished apartment where nothing belonged to them, just as nothing had ever really belonged to them, for that matter, anywhere they'd lived, among the books, the decorative objects, the paintings bought as a job lot that gradually got covered in dust, beneath the electric chandeliers where half the light bulbs needed replacing, and which cast a dim, yellowish glow. Roses no one tended died in their vases; a piano whose cover was never raised by anyone had been pushed into a corner, between torn lace curtains that had cost a thousand francs a metre and were now full of cigarette burns. The carpets were covered in ash; the scornful, silent servants set down the coffee on a corner of the desk and disappeared, their bitter smiles passing harsh judgement on these 'mad foreigners'. It never crossed Hélène's mind that she herself might be able to bring a little order and harmony to this home. She was too used to setting up camp wherever they landed to consider the furniture or ornaments as her own; everything, even the curtains and books that decorated her bedroom, aroused a feeling of hostility and mistrust within her.

'What's the point? As soon as I get attached to anything, something will surely happen and we'll have to leave.'

Whenever Karol won at the club he was as joyous and mischievous as a child; he would tell stories about his poor but happy childhood; Hélène listened as if these stories touched a chord in her blood. When she closed her eyes she felt as if she had lived in those dark streets herself, played in the mud and dust, slept at the back of one of those little shops her father described where, in winter, they put a lit candle in front of the window to melt the ice.

Bella, who was too nervous to sit still, but whose hands were never busy doing anything useful, was unstitching dresses; they had been delivered that morning; they came from Chanel or Patou; by the evening they were nothing more than a pile of fabric and crumpled lace.

Bella didn't notice the way Max stared at Hélène. She

didn't hear how his voice faltered, didn't worry about the strangely sweet expression that appeared on his face, the slight trembling of his hands if he accidentally brushed against Hélène's bare arm. To her, Hélène would be a child until the day she died.

'This is the land of make-believe,' thought Hélène. 'Papa plays with paper and pretends it's money. We entertain all the hoi polloi in Paris and call them society. I'm not allowed to cut my hair, it's all the way down my back, and she thinks that will do it, that I'll be twelve years old for ever and that Max will never notice that I'm a woman. Just you wait, you old hag, just you wait . . .'

One evening after Karol had left for the club, as he did every night, the clock struck eleven and Bella called to Max, 'Shall we go out? It's such a nice evening. Let's go to the Bois de Boulogne.'

It was a beautiful spring night. Max agreed. Bella went to get her hat. Suddenly Hélène took the young man's hand and said, 'I don't want you to go out.'

'Why not?' he whispered.

'I don't want you to,' she said again, pleading and capricious.

They looked at each other for a long time and there passed between them the silent consent that ties a man to a woman, when, even though not a word has been said, a kiss given or received, everything is understood, silently spoken, with no turning back.

Nevertheless, the profound effect of his love for Bella remained within him. Her dominating personality, her whims, her madness, everything that had aroused in him deep, sensual, painful feelings of love and desire, had gradually ebbed away;

but just as a wave recedes, leaving the beach vulnerable for a stronger wave to crash over it, so a new love had washed over him, a twin of his old love, bringing in its wake the same jealousy, the same tyranny, the same cruel and agonising tenderness.

'Why?' he asked again, without looking at her, but with a powerful rush of blood to his face that reached right up to his sunken temples.

'I'm bored. Oh, Max, I was so bored because of you when I was a child. Don't you want to give in to my whim a little now?' she said softly.

He looked at her cruelly, then quickly turned away. 'Very well, but you'll also indulge me when I want, then . . .'

'What do you mean?'

He saw she had moved away and forced himself to laugh. 'I was joking, of course,' he whispered.

When Bella came back, he told her he wouldn't be going out and he spent the rest of the time smoking nervously, putting out half-finished cigarettes one after the other. He looked exhausted, pale, anxious. Finally he left. Hélène heard the sound of the large door close behind him in the empty street. Bella had sat down and didn't move, her eyes full of tears, staring blankly in front of her.

Hélène crossed the room and leaned against the ledge by the open window; moonlight shone down on the street; a tree, its first leaves just beginning to grow, swayed its delicate, supple branches. She looked at the Eiffel Tower where a sign flashed: *Citroën, Citroën.* 'I'm so happy,' she thought with surprise, 'although there's nothing to be happy about . . .'

Hélène's black cat, Tintabel, sat on the balcony railing;

Max had given him to her and he was the one thing she loved most in the world after her father, and the only thing she could stroke, take care of and keep close to her. Sometimes she would hold him tightly and say, 'I love you, yes, I do. You're warm and alive and I love you.'

He raised his face towards the moon.

'I'm happy because I've got what I wanted, because Max loves me,' she mused. For she knew very well that he did love her, yet the ease with which she had won him left her feeling disappointed and embarrassed.

'No, it's not that. It's everything, it's surely because I'm young,' she thought, savouring the pleasure of being eighteen which, for her, wasn't about the intoxication and exhilaration of youth, but rather a sensation of well-being, of having a supple, strong body, young blood that flowed peacefully and joyously through her veins. She raised her beautiful arms into the air: they were delicate with soft skin; her hands were agile and slim. She looked at the pale reflection of her body and face in the mirror and was pleased. The cat came and rubbed his smooth black head up against her, purring.

She whistled in the particular way he recognised and which made him meow softly with joy and affection.

'Tintabel . . .'

She bent her head and let her long hair fall down into the darkness. She liked watching the sleepy town with its little flickering lights; she liked breathing in the gentle night breeze that carried the scent of the Bois de Boulogne.

On a bench outside a man and a woman were kissing. She watched them with curiosity and scorn.

'Love is ugly and stupid. But what about Fred? Oh, Fred. That was just a bit of fun.'

'Tintabel,' she said to the cat, 'how wise we become when we grow up.'

She leaned out over the edge of the balcony, swaying absent-mindedly, enjoying the dangerous pleasure of being half suspended in mid-air, and she thought she could hear a beloved voice, silent now.

'Lili, you mustn't do that. You shouldn't play dangerous games, that's not what real courage is.'

But those words had a meaning she didn't want to understand. 'Real courage? Yes, I know: being humble, forgiving. But no, no . . . you can't ask me to do that, really, you can't ask me to do such a thing. First of all, when I decide the game has lasted long enough I'll stop. But not before I've made *her* suffer. At least a little, and it will always be less than I suffered because of her. Just let her suffer a little . . .'

She turned round, looked at her mother for a long time, cruelly, screwing up her eyes. 'What a beautiful night,' she said. 'How wonderful it is to be eighteen! Oh, I wouldn't like to be old, Mama . . . my poor Mama.'

Bella shuddered; Hélène saw her hands tremble, the hands she hated so much: her nails were still shaped like claws but had lost their strength and brightness over the years. 'You'll get old just like everyone else, my girl,' she said, her voice low and faint, 'then you'll see how amusing it is.'

'Oh, but I still have time on my side,' Hélène said happily, 'lots of time . . .'

Bella stood up and left the room, slamming the door angrily behind her.

When she was alone, Hélène could feel tears welling up in her eyes in spite of herself. 'So,' she thought, shrugging her shoulders, 'do I feel sorry for her? No, and besides, it's not my fault that she's getting old. All she had to do was not take up with a gigolo fifteen years younger than she was. But I, I . . . I'm just as bad as they are.'

# 4

Slowly, gradually, the guilty love grew stronger. It had already set its deep, sinuous roots into the man's heart before the first fragile flower had started to bloom. It seemed so delicate, so small, that the man thought about it less to admire it than to become intoxicated by its very power. Its perfume was so strong. Yet it would take the slightest gesture, the tiniest effort to pluck it out, to kill it for ever in his soul, and it would all be over. So what did he have to fear? He smiled with defiance and tenderness. 'Well, then, all right, so it's the beginning of love. What do I have to fear, at my age? I know that if I let it grow, it will only bring me unhappiness.' But from the day he called it love, when he consented to acknowledge it existed, he became aware of his own weakness for the first time. Agile, tenacious roots plunged deeper and deeper within him with every passing day. The moment when he finally shuddered and thought 'That's enough now, enough, the game is over' was the very moment when he succumbed, when he got used to being in love, when he cherished his suffering. Then all he could do was wait, wait for time and disillusionment to destroy the deep-rooted, fragile, deadly flower.

Max had begun to think about Hélène, picturing her face when he was in bed at night, when he felt particularly tired of his ageing mistress and life itself. Just before falling asleep, he liked to close his eyes and imagine Hélène's face. He wasn't in love. How absurd! 'Ah,' he thought, 'never again. Love, how ridiculous. Love is a terrible cross to bear. In love with Hélène, with that child?' He remembered one day in autumn, on the islands in St Petersburg, when he'd been out walking with Bella; he'd noticed how little Hélène was dragging her boots through the mud and looking gloomy. How he'd hated her! Her very presence irritated him. Every time she looked at him, he felt she was spying on him. How many times had he said to Bella, 'But really, why don't you dump her in some boarding school so she leaves us in peace?' That little girl . . . And now? No, no, he didn't love her. His imagination was playing tricks on him, it was a whim. Except he enjoyed seeing her so much. And she was the only person in the world he could talk to honestly, as a friend. He thought back to her thin, sun-tanned neck, her face, so young . . . Young, that was what he found so seductive. He was thirty and Bella . . . 'Wooden dolls, lifeless and cold,' Bella said of younger women. 'Two a penny . . .' True, but older women in love were intense, passionate creatures, and were they so very difficult to find? Sometimes, when he was asleep, some quirk merged the faces of the two women. Sometimes he was holding Hélène tightly in his arms but calling her: 'Bella, darling Bella . . .'

Then he would wake up shaking, his heart gripped with disgust and shame, thinking, 'I don't love her. I'm playing at love. I'm amusing myself. It will be over for ever whenever I want . . .'

Time passed, however, and he could no longer fool himself. 'My mistress's daughter,' he thought with terror and remorse.

Well, so what? It wasn't unusual.

'It's almost inevitable,' he thought. 'it . . . happens all the time. Bella will never forgive us. She's not a mother, not Bella, she's wholly and ferociously a woman. Well, then, so she won't forgive us, I don't really give a damn. After all, I gave her my best years. Isn't that enough? I gave up my mother, my family, my youth for her . . .'

He had loved her so much, this woman who, even then, wasn't young or beautiful. But she knew how to give pleasure. He recalled the angry scenes with his mother, his sisters' tears. They had tried everything (such clumsy attempts!) to tear him away from 'that woman'. He could still remember the tone of his mother's voice as she said, 'She doesn't love you. She just wanted to get revenge on me, take you away from me. You poor boy. She was nothing, *a mere nobody*,' she would say in English, bitterly, finding some consolation in being able to speak that language fluently, unlike Bella who had undoubtedly only learned it from some lover she once had: 'She's so smug now, smug because she took my son away from me; that woman I refused to receive, not because she was poor, thank God! I'm above anything like that. But because she behaved like a slut. That viper! She took my son! Do you think she did it for any other reason? Believe me, my boy, women don't love a man for himself but as a weapon against another woman.'

'Yes,' Max mused, 'she was right . . .'

He was old enough, however, to realise that love was rarely pure and simple at the beginning. At first, Bella had wanted to take her revenge on Madame Safronov. But later she had loved him as faithfully as a woman like her was capable of loving. What he hadn't known was that his youth and his excessive passion satisfied in her a sensual need for love that was full of danger, a kind of love that one of her former lovers had kindled in her heart.

'She wanted me to live and breathe only because of her. I'm all alone in the world now, with her . . .'

He felt his solitude as pain, a feeling of suffocation that was almost physical. 'I haven't a single friend, apart from Hélène. To Bella, relationships, simple human relationships, family ties, friendships, companionship, don't exist. A friend, a family, a home, I miss all those things and will miss them for ever, as long as I stay with her.' He sometimes thought of leaving her. But life without the Karols seemed impossible to him. He had no one but them. He felt tied to them as much by his desire for pleasure as by simple human habit. He feared an even more bitter feeling of solitude, one that was irreversible. Sometimes he would go for days on end without answering the telephone or replying to Bella's messages. But he was too often bored in this foreign country, with no friends, no profession. He had brought a fortune from Russia that was neither great enough to allow him expensive distractions nor small enough to make him feel he needed to work for a living. He wanted to see Hélène again. He went back. He watched her coming and going, running and jumping with an elegant lightness given wings by her extreme youth; it seemed almost impossible to keep her on the ground.

'How young you are, my God,' he whispered with astonishment, bitterness and envious despair. 'You're so young!'

He took her hand, secretly pressed it against his cheek
with a shy, innocent gesture.

One June day the Karols were having lunch at Max's house.
They were all about to leave for Biarritz. Max lived in a
modest, quiet little apartment in a peaceful street in Passy;
it was almost like living in the countryside. A storm was
brewing over Paris; the sky was covered in copper-coloured
wisps of cloud that slowly moved closer together to form
a blanket of pink mist that parted every so often to reveal a
dazzling ray of light.

When lunch was over, Max went out to buy a small suitcase
he needed. Hélène picked up a book.

Karol stared nostalgically at some invisible point in the
distance. His fingers were never still; he snapped them loudly
and rhythmically, like castanets. Hélène realised that he was
imagining the gaming table at the club. He finally stood up
and sighed. 'I didn't have time to shave. I'll be back in half
an hour . . .'

'But Boris,' his wife cried, 'we're leaving as soon as Max
gets back! Come on, you know if you go out you won't come
back until tonight.'

'Don't be silly,' said Boris Karol and his face lit up with
that mischievous smile Hélène loved so much. 'Here, my
darling,' he said, slipping some money into his wife's hand,
'you have just enough time to buy yourself that new hat you
wanted.'

She softened.

'Let's go downstairs together.'

Hélène was alone. A gentle breeze rustled the branches of

a nearby tree; the stormy sun appeared, lighting up the leaves that strained in the wind. The clouds got darker, blocking out the light, the tree swayed and creaked as the wind ripped off the young June leaves, still so green and delicate.

The key turned in the lock and Max came in. He wasn't surprised to find the house empty. He knew what the Karols were like. He waited. At around four o'clock Karol, whom no one had expected to see before evening, arrived at the house. He slammed the door angrily.

'My wife isn't back yet? I told her to wait for me in the car. When I came out she was gone. That's so like her. She made me give my word that I wouldn't stay at the club for more than half an hour and, just when my luck was beginning to change, she disappears.'

'But my poor friend,' said Max, his voice weary, 'it's after four o'clock. She must have waited for you for two and a half hours. You have to admit that . . .'

Karol wasn't listening; he was shaking with impatience, watching the door; his eyes shone, but with a sad, passionate, gloomy look. 'My God,' he said, 'what a shame. Just when my luck was starting to change . . .'

He paced up and down the room.

'I'm going back to the club,' he said at last, forcing himself to laugh. 'I'll be back in a flash.'

'It's going to rain, Papa,' cried Hélène, 'and you don't have a raincoat. Wait a moment, take an umbrella, you were coughing so much yesterday . . .'

'Don't make a fuss,' he shouted happily as he disappeared. 'I've seen worse.'

'Where's the other one now?' said Max, shaking with annoyance. 'It's nearly five o'clock.'

Hélène started to laugh. 'My dear Max. Haven't you learned by now? We'll leave this evening, or in the middle of the night, or tomorrow, or next week. What's the difference? Will it be any better or different from being here?'

He didn't reply. They were alone. The clock ticked. Far off in the distance thunder rumbled in the skies with the deep, soft sound of a bird cooing.

The telephone rang. Max answered it.

'Hello, yes, it's me . . .'

Hélène recognised her mother's voice.

'He came back and then went out again,' Max said. 'No,' he continued, hesitating, 'she's not here either. I'm going out. I can see the trip is off. Let's go tomorrow.'

He hung up and stood there, gloomy and silent.

Hélène looked at him and smiled. 'Telling lies, my little Max?'

'Oh, for God's sake!' he replied. 'Let's just have a moment's peace for once.'

The first heavy, large drops of rain pattered against the windows. It was dark outside now. Hélène shuddered. 'It's so cold all of a sudden, for June. It must be hailing . . .'

'Let's close the shutters,' he said.

With the shutters and curtains closed, and a small lamp switched on in the darkness, the little room felt peaceful and friendly.

'Come on, let's have something to eat.'

They put some water on to boil. Hélène set the table. She walked over to a pink vase that had carnations in it. 'Max, you haven't even taken off the metal bands from the florist, you bad boy. The rust will kill your flowers.'

She cut off some of the stems, changed the water,

maliciously enjoying the look of pleasure that spread across Max's face.

'I need a woman here,' he said innocently.

Rainwater flowed down the empty street. In the next room the blinds were open and they could see shining, light sprays of water swirling over the pavement in the wind.

Max closed the door. There wasn't a single sound now. He sat down at her feet. 'Wait, don't move, let me help you, let me serve you. Would you like some tea? There's a cake left from breakfast. You can have it. Please have it.'

Humble and attentive, he watched her as she ate, his amorous eyes fixed on her white teeth that shone between her lips. The profound stillness held them in a kind of sweet, silent spell.

'I find you so attractive,' he said finally, so quietly that he had to say it again before she could understand his words. He was trembling.

'At last,' she mused, mocking herself as much as him. 'Here it is. The moment I've waited for so long.'

How had she managed it? She remembered the hills in Finland, when the slightest push sent the sleigh flying off into space. She had set everything in motion the first time she'd smiled at him on the boat, when she'd spoken to him without letting him see how much she hated him, and after that moment her persistent presence had affected him so quickly, so imperceptibly, that he'd felt the kind of intangible enchantment that grows between a man and a woman who are constantly together even though they aren't related.

Gently, she stroked his face; she felt a friendly, vague sense of pity for him; she was so strong, so serene, so sure of her power; but then she frowned and pulled her hand away.

Wishing to see him tremble and look up at her with an expression of fear and submission, she said, 'Leave me alone.'

'Hélène,' he said quickly, his voice hoarse, 'I love you, I want to marry you. I love you, my darling Hélène . . .'

'What are you saying?'

She had cried out in surprise and with a kind of hatred and bitterness that shocked him. 'Never,' she whispered, 'never, never, never . . .'

'Why not?' he said, anger flashing in his eyes, which brought back the Max she had so detested, the enemy of her childhood; she shrugged her shoulders, wanting to say 'Because I don't love you'. But she immediately thought, 'Ah, no. If I tell him that he'll never forgive me, it will be finished, the game will be over. Marry him? I'd never do anything as stupid as that. My desire for revenge isn't strong enough to risk my own happiness. I don't love him . . .'

She just shook her head in silence.

He thought he understood and went deathly pale. He grabbed her and held her in his arms. 'Hélène, forgive me, forgive me, how could I know? I love you, you're still so young, you'll love me some day. It isn't possible that you won't love me,' he said, as she allowed him to kiss her cheek and lips in passionate despair.

Outside, the loud noise of the rain was subsiding; they could hear the faint musical sound of the dripping wet leaves more clearly. Max held her tightly against him, and she could feel his mouth trembling as he gently kissed and bit her shoulder through the flimsy fabric of her dress.

Gently she pushed him away. 'No, no . . .'

He wanted to kiss her on the lips but she stretched out her hands and thrust away his eager, affectionate face.

'Let go of me! I can hear footsteps; it's my mother,' she cried, terrified.

He let her go; she fell back on to the settee, pale and drained. But it was only the driver who had come up to find out what he should do. While Max was talking to him, she slipped out of the room and ran away.

# 5

They didn't leave for Biarritz that night; Hélène went home. She got into her narrow bed; her room was the only one on the ground floor of the house they lived in and her bed was pushed up against the window. Noise from the city beat against her shutters while, above her head, she heard her mother walking endlessly from one room to another in an attempt to overcome her insomnia and stop herself from crying; outside, she could hear cars coming back from the countryside; couples who had stayed out late strolled down the street or kissed on benches. Hélène lit the lamp; she looked at the décor of her life with hostility: the bright red and sea-green Directoire mouldings, the pink curtains, the tall, narrow mirrors set into the walls. She loved nothing in this world.

'Nothing and no one,' she thought sadly. 'I should have been so happy tonight. I got everything I desired. If only I wanted to . . .'

She shook her head and laughed.

'Oh Hélène,' she said, talking to herself as she had done

since she was a child, 'you know very well that you're the
strongest one and they're nothing but pitifully easy prey.
Was it really so difficult to make Max fall in love with you?
I'm eighteen and she's forty-five. Any young girl could have
done it. And here you are, bursting with pride. What you
should have done was conquer yourself. What right do you
have to look at them with scorn if you're no stronger, no
better than they are?' She raised her slim, tanned arm and
looked at the veins visible beneath the skin. 'I've spent my
whole life fighting against my hideous bloodline,' she
thought, 'but it's here within me. It's flowing through me,
and if I don't learn how to conquer myself, this bitter, cursed
blood will win out.'

She recalled the mirror in the dark room at Max's apartment and how her face looked when she let him kiss her. It
was a terrifying, sensual, triumphant face, and for an instant
it reminded her of the way her mother had looked when she
was young.

'I won't let this demon get the better of me,' she said out
loud, laughing. 'Surely it's easy to give up the game, now
that I virtually have what I set out to get. I'm not a hypocrite, I don't make myself out to be better than I am; I'm
not good, I don't want to be good. Being good has something
soft, weak, suffocating about it. But I do want to be stronger
than I am, to conquer myself. Yes, to leave them in their
mire, with their shame, while I . . . My God,' she murmured
with sudden, heart-rending remorse, 'I'm so flawed, so bitter,
so egotistical, so proud of myself. I have no humility, no
charity in my heart, but I want so very much to be better. I
swear that from this day forward he'll never see me alone.
I'll avoid him. I'll avoid him with as much determination as

I did before when trying to arrange to be alone with him. It will be boring.' She smiled. 'Well, too bad! It's what I want. Demon of pride or demon of vengeance, we'll see which is the stronger! But will I have the courage to see her happy? Yes, why not? From this moment on I'll no longer hate her. I've forgiven her . . .'

She threw off her blanket and stretched out straight, with her arms under her head.

'Yes, it's odd, but for the first time in my life I can think of her without my heart quivering or feeling as heavy as stone. I even feel a little sorry for her . . .'

She pictured her mother's pale face, the marks her tears left on her make-up, her ravaged features.

'Me, her little Hélène . . . What did she call me? "An awkward, wild little girl. You're so clumsy, my poor Hélène."'

Her eyes flashed in the darkness.

'Not as clumsy as all that,' she whispered, clenching her teeth, but she forced herself to slow the intense, rapid beating of her heart. 'Being a hungry wolf isn't all that hard but it's not worthy of me. I'll tell Max that I don't love him, that it was all just a game. He'll go back to her, even if it's only to try to make me suffer. Tomorrow, everything will go back to normal, so to speak. Since Father either doesn't see anything or doesn't want to see anything, all I have to do is let things carry on as they were. And besides, my intense, evil pleasure was poisoned by bitterness. What a strange night.' She switched off the lamp and watched silvery rays of light peek through the shutters. 'What beautiful moonlight . . .'

She got out of bed and walked barefoot over to the window; she opened the shutters and looked out at the wide, empty avenue. The wind was blowing in from the Bois. The night was crystal clear now, a transparent blue. She sat down by the window, humming softly. Never had her heart felt so light; a kind of joyous passion flowed through her blood. 'To know that I'm the one who holds her happiness in my hands and can manipulate it as I wish . . . Isn't that the best revenge? What more could I want? I don't love him. If I did love him . . .'

She stared straight ahead, picturing in her mind his eager, submissive face. 'I don't love anyone, thank God, I'm alone and free. If I could,' she suddenly thought, 'I'd go away right now, tonight. To tell the truth, that's all I really want. To go away to some corner of the earth where I'll never see my mother or this house ever again, where I'll never hear the word "money", or the word "love". But there's my father . . . Although, he doesn't need me,' she thought bitterly. 'No one needs me. Max is in love, but that's not what I need, I want a peaceful, secure kind of tenderness. But do I really? I'm not a child any more. I'm at the age where most people reject that kind of tenderness . . . Yes, but I've never had it, I've missed it so much . . . And not having had a childhood when I should have means that it's probably impossible to mature like other people; I'm shrivelled on one side and green on the other, like fruit that's been exposed to the cold and the wind.'

It was almost as if the recent years of sadness had melted away and she was, once again, the strong, powerful child who silently choked back her tears, clenched her fists and used all her strength to suffer without a word of complaint.

'Life is beautiful but harsh,' she said out loud.

She'd gone back to bed, but left the shutters open; she watched the night grow lighter and the spring morning glisten on the leaves. Finally, she fell asleep.

# 6

A week went by during which Hélène succeeded in avoiding Max, but their lives were too closely intertwined by Bella's will and their chaotic lifestyle. She missed him already, especially towards the end of the day. On those interminable evenings when, at nine or ten o'clock, they were still waiting for Karol to arrive home so they could sit down to dinner, Hélène felt so sad that she thought about Max, wanting him to be there in spite of herself. Kneeling on a chair, she absent-mindedly sketched the contours of the rickety old Louis XV desk whose decorative gilt claws were hanging loose; above her head she heard the butler's impatient footsteps. The situation awakened too many memories in her heart . . .

One evening Madame Karol, holding the telephone in one hand, flew through the room where Hélène was, followed by a chambermaid who was trying to shorten her dress; her mouth full of pins, the servant stumbled as her feet got caught up in the telephone wire; behind her was another servant, carrying a jewellery box with the lid open.

Hélène heard her mother calling Max's number. While she

was speaking, Bella was putting on her diamond earrings; she dropped them and they rolled on to the floor. She was speaking in Russian and stopped every now and again, presumably because she remembered that Hélène was in the next room, but then she forgot again and began pleading once more: 'Do come, please come . . . You promised you'd go out with me tonight . . . He's not here, I'm so lonely, Max . . . Take pity on me . . .'

After she hung up, she stood still for a moment, absent-mindedly wringing her hands. It was over. He didn't love her any more. Anxiously she searched her memory to see which woman could have stolen him from her. He was tired of her.

'In the past we quarrelled, but he always came back to me more submissive and loving. In the past . . . it's barely been a year . . . but now . . . Oh, another woman has stolen him, I can feel it,' she thought with despair. 'What will I do without him?'

She remembered with profound bitterness how she had been scrupulous about being faithful to him.

'My best years are gone . . . I don't want to admit it, so I show off, but I know very well that youth and love are finished for me now. It's either that or paying for lovers, gigolos, young boys you keep, who are young enough to be your son, and who make fun of you behind your back.' She pictured some of her women friends with the handsome young men they kept on a leash like a Pekinese. 'Or perhaps I should just give in, become an old woman. Oh no, no, never that, never! I can't do without love, it isn't possible,' she murmured and, instinctively, she wiped away the tears that ran down her neck through her pearls.

'He's decked me out with jewels as if I were a shrine,' she thought, hearing the door open and the sound of her husband's footsteps in the next room, 'but that's not what I need, and besides, I'm bored, I'm so terribly bored. If you don't have a man in your life, if you don't have a young, handsome lover, what's the point of living? Women who claim to be satisfied without love are either ignorant, fools or hypocrites. I need love,' she said urgently, looking at her distorted face in the mirror with hatred. 'If they only knew how clearly I see myself, without pity, without being indulgent.'

They sat down to dinner. The windowless hall had been transformed into a dining room; it was cold and gloomy with a bluish cast; dust gathered on the imitation marble mouldings.

Fancy stucco work reigned supreme; the carpet had blue and white squares in imitation of stone tiles; the artificial flowers in marble urns were covered with mildew and gave off the slightly acrid odour of dust; alabaster fruits sat in a conch shell, an electric light illuminating them from within. The marble table was so cold that it froze your hands through the lace doilies. Karol ate eagerly, hurriedly; he swallowed his food without seeing it or tasting it and, along with it, the many tablets he was given, which he hoped would allow him to do without rest and fresh air. Hélène studied him with silent pity: he was more handsome and more elegant than ever.

He was blessed with a fire, a kind of touching passion that burned with the greatest beauty just as it was about to die down. In his pale, tormented face, his beautiful, piercing sad eyes were covered by a yellowish film, yet shone with a brightness that was almost unbearable. He continually snapped his thin fingers: 'Faster, come on, serve up faster . . .'

'Are you going out again tonight?' Bella sighed.

'I have a business meeting. But you're going out as well, aren't you?' he asked, looking at her.

She shook her head. 'No.'

Then, immediately, she continued in a bitter, pleading voice, 'I'm always alone. The life we lead is mad. I'm the unhappiest woman in the world. I've always suffered.'

He didn't reply. He was barely listening to her; after twenty years of married life he was used to her complaining.

But that evening Hélène was prepared to feel sorry for her; she was an ageing, argumentative woman who sat opposite her but never looked at her, as if the sight of her young face was too painful; her beautiful hands and bare arms covered in bracelets rested sadly on the tablecloth. Her face was painted, bloated, heavy with make-up and sticky from all the powder and cream, but it seemed as if her flesh was giving way from the inside, and that its smooth, pink-and-white surface was slowly sagging, revealing the ravages of age; yet she still had a wonderful figure, with pert, firm breasts.

Hélène turned towards her father. 'Papa, darling Papa, do stay home tonight. Look at you. You look so tired . . .'

He shrugged his shoulders; when she insisted and Bella began complaining again he cried out impatiently, 'To hell with all you women!'

Hélène fell silent, her eyes welling up with tears: it hurt that he rejected her like that and especially that he treated her the same as her mother. 'Can't he see that I love him?' she wondered sadly.

But all he could see was the green gaming table where that very night he would lose a fortune.

'No,' thought Hélène, 'it's not so easy to give up Max, or to stop gambling.'

The next day, quite suddenly, they left for Biarritz; Hélène had no excuses to allow her to remain in Paris; besides, they still treated her like a little girl who had no business questioning what she was told to do, and Max was going with them.

In the morning, in Blois, he called her down while Bella was still asleep and bought her some of the first cherries of the season from an outdoor stall on a little street rosy with sunshine; the fruit was covered by a silvery dew and as icy cold and delicious as a drop of chilled liqueur. He looked at her with desire and tenderness. 'Hélène, you are so elusive, evasive, enigmatic, I find you so attractive, so very attractive. I've never loved another woman the way I love you. You're beautiful, I'm mad about you . . .'

All those old words of love that, to her, were so new went straight to her heart, in spite of herself.

'I don't have the courage,' she thought. 'It's not hard to conquer the demon of sensuality, but the demon of flirtatiousness, of cruelty, of the pleasure in playing with a man's love for the very first time . . .

'I wouldn't have the courage,' she said to herself again; she made a superhuman effort, lowered her eyes and thought, with the black humour she had inherited from her father, 'I'm earning my place in heaven . . .'

She replied to him in a calm, measured voice. 'Max, don't. I don't love you, I was playing at being in love.' But she was really thinking, 'Hypocrite, that will only make him want you more.'

He turned white, looked at her harshly and suddenly, she was afraid of losing him. It was all so amusing, after all.

'And why give him up? To avoid hurting a woman I've always hated? I don't want to! I'm having fun!' She felt a strong wave of pride and pleasure surge through her heart; gently she took his hand. 'There, there, what a terrible look . . . I was teasing you.'

He shuddered when she touched him and looked at her childlike face with its womanly expression almost with fear. He wanted her so much. He loved every one of her gestures, still gauche and awkward, her long hair floating over her slim shoulders, her delicate neck, her thick eyelashes and dazzling eyes that retained a look of pride and childlike innocence, her long legs, strong fingers, the shy, capricious way she pulled away from his embrace, her sweet breath . . . They were alone; he leaned towards her, put his arms round her and said softly, 'Kiss me.'

She quickly kissed him on the cheek and he felt a kind of uneasy emotion; she kissed like a little girl, but the way she let him kiss her, silently closing her eyes, was like a woman . . .

'What am I doing?' Hélène thought.

But it was too late to stop the game.

It was only when they got back to Paris that Hélène realised how much power Max had over her. He was becoming as tyrannical, jealous and cruel towards her as he'd been with Bella in the past. Men learn how to love, just as they learn everything, and the method they use never changes; it's the same with every woman, in spite of themselves.

'Marry me,' he kept saying. 'You're unhappy living at home.'

She refused. He would then fly into a rage that left him pale and trembling as he swore at her. He knew very well that she was toying with him, but that knowledge was no longer enough to keep him calm; he entered into that phase of unrequited love that resembles mournful folly and Hélène watched in consternation at the madness she had unleashed within him; it was eating him up and she couldn't understand it. The first time she said, without thinking 'If my mother knew . . .' he burst out laughing.

'Tell her, go on, tell her. You'll see how wonderful your life will be then, my girl. She'll never forgive you, never. You're still only a child, a kid. She'll make you pay, and dearly . . .'

Meanwhile, he continued his affair with Bella for so many reasons. He took his frustration with Hélène out on her, venting his irritation and using her to satisfy his mad desire, since Hélène refused his caresses, which filled her with horror and repulsion. 'It's your fault,' he would say in despair, 'it's all your fault. I'm offering you a proper, normal life and you're refusing.'

In the evening he made Bella come to his flat so he could safely telephone Hélène, since he knew she'd be alone at home. Bella would come home at midnight looking pale and haggard; but the next day she would go back when he called and Hélène would tremble as she waited for the ringing telephone to echo through the empty apartment.

Hunched over, her eyes staring blankly out into space, pressing her trembling hand to her cheek, she would wait, without the strength to run away and free herself from temptation.

The telephone rang; she picked up the receiver and heard Max's voice.

'When will you come? Why did you let me kiss you if you don't love me? I'll do whatever you want. Just come. I won't touch you. I'm begging you to come.'

'No, no, no,' she would reply, feeling her blood run icy cold. She turned towards the door, afraid that her father, her mother, the servants, would hear what she was saying, while Max, in despair, endlessly repeated the same things, his voice sounding tender and bitter both at once. He seemed to hiss out each word.

'My darling, my darling, my darling Hélène, come to me, come, have pity on me . . .'

Then, suddenly, he stopped and hung up; she heard the little clicking noise that ended the connection.

'She's just arrived,' she thought, angry and in pain. 'She's ringing the bell. He's going to answer it and . . . but I'm not jealous! I was supposed to win . . . But I wanted this . . . it's my fault.' Then she tried to laugh through her tears. 'It's what you wanted, Georges Dandin,' she said, thinking of the Molière play, ashamed at being so upset. 'What have I done? And where will I find the courage, my Lord, to conquer myself and to forgive, to forget, to leave vengeance only to God?'

And as soon as she was in bed, about to fall into that peaceful, contented sleep she had retained from her childhood, which invariably took her back to memories long past, joyous and innocent, the telephone would ring again, pull her out of bed and once more she would hear that loving, evil voice.

'Hélène, Hélène, I want to hear your voice. I can't sleep

until I've heard your voice. Say something, just one word, make a promise, even if you don't keep it, tell me you'll love me one day.' Then suddenly he would shout in a fit of blind anger, 'Be careful, I can hurt you; I want to kill you!'

'You're behaving like a child,' she replied, shrugging her shoulders.

'Well, then, leave me in peace,' he cried in despair. 'Why were you always hanging around me? You're nothing but a stupid kid, a liar and a flirt! I don't love you, I couldn't care less about you, I . . . No, Hélène, don't leave me, forgive me, I'm begging you to come, just once. When I feel your young, smooth cheek beneath my lips, it drives me mad. Hélène. My darling, my darling, my darling . . .'

Hélène heard the sound of the main gate opening outside her window. 'Let me go now,' she whispered. 'Let me go. I can't talk any more.'

A sense of decency prevented her from saying, 'My mother's home.'

But he had no trouble understanding and, happy to be the stronger, the one to be feared, at least for a moment, he replied, 'Good! If you don't swear that you'll come and see me tomorrow, I'll keep calling all night long until your mother hears the phone. Don't push me too far, Hélène, you don't really know me. I've known how to manipulate other women!'

'But they loved you.'

'Fine, I'll call all night long then, do you hear me? Your mother will find out everything, and your father, Hélène? He'll find out everything, you understand what I'm saying? Everything. The past and the present. It's monstrous, I know that very well, but it's your fault, you're forcing me to behave this way! Listen to me, just promise. Just this once! I love you! Take pity on me!'

Hélène heard her mother's footsteps outside her bedroom. She heard the door open where Karol was asleep. 'I promise,' she whispered.

# 7

One rainy day the two of them were driving through the Bois de Boulogne with no specific destination in mind, just happy to take refuge in the damp, deserted lanes where they wouldn't run into anyone they knew. It was autumn, the beginning of October; they could hear bursts of heavy, cold rain beating against the windows. Sometimes the driver would stop, shrug his shoulders and look at Max. Max tapped on the window impatiently. 'Keep going. Wherever you like.'

The car continued on its way; every now and again it got stuck in the mud on the horse trails. After a while they crossed the Seine and found themselves in the countryside; a cool, bitter scent filtered in through the open windows. Hélène looked at the man sitting next to her as if she were in some embarrassing nightmare: he was crying and talking to her without even bothering to wipe away his tears. She felt both pity and repugnance towards him.

'Hélène, you must try to understand me. I can't go on living like this. We've never talked about *her*,' he said, to avoid saying the name of his mistress. 'What I'm doing is horrible. But it's better to talk about it and be done with it once and for all. You . . . you've . . . known about our affair for a long time, haven't you?'

'Oh, for heaven's sake!' she said, shrugging her shoulders. 'Didn't you realise that even when I was a child I would have had to be blind and a fool not to guess what was going on?'

'Do you believe that anyone gives a thought to children?' he exclaimed, and for a moment she saw his face contort with scorn and weariness, the way it used to; she could feel the past hatred stirring in her heart.

'I know very well that no one ever thinks about children,' she murmured.

'But what has that got to do with it? We're talking about you now, a woman I love and a woman I once loved, sincerely loved. I can't continue betraying her like this. I've lived through these past few months as if I were in some depressing nightmare. I feel as if I'm waking up. I understand how horrible and miserable I've been. Or rather, I knew very well how I felt, but I couldn't stop myself, I loved you too much, I was mad,' he said softly, 'but I can't carry on like this, I hate myself.'

'You betrayed my father for years with no remorse,' she said bitterly.

'Your father?' he murmured, 'Do you know what he thinks? Has anyone ever known what he was thinking? You're fooling yourself if you think you know him. As for me, I have no idea what he knows or doesn't know. Hélène, if you wanted . . .'

'Wanted what?' she asked, pulling her hand away from his burning cheek.

'Marry me, Hélène, you'll be happy.'

She slowly shook her head.

'Why not?' he said in despair.

'I don't love you. You are the enemy of my entire child-hood. I can't explain it. You've just said: "It has nothing to do with you when you were a child." But it does, it does have to do with that. I'll never change. The feelings I had when I was fourteen – even younger . . . much younger – are and will always be the same. I could never forget, never. I could never, ever be happy living with you. I want to live with a man who's never known my mother, or my house, who doesn't even come from the same country or speak the same language, someone who will take me far away, anywhere, miles from anywhere, just far away from here. I'd be unhappy with you even if I did love you. But I don't.'

He clenched his fists in fury. 'You let me kiss you . . .'

'What has that got to do with love?' she said wearily.

'In that case I want to go away. My sister is in London. She's written to ask me to come and join her. I want to go away,' he said again, groaning.

'Well, then, go, my dear Max.'

'Hélène, if I leave you'll never see me again. You might need a friend one day. Think about it; you have no one in the world apart from your father. He's old and ill . . .'

She shuddered. 'Papa? What do you mean?'

'Come on now,' he said, shrugging his shoulders. 'Have you looked at him? He's finished. Worn out. What will you do then? You and your mother will always be enemies.'

'Always,' she echoed, 'but I don't need anyone.'

'I feel as if I haven't felt any true emotions in ten years,' he said in despair. 'I'm ashamed of myself. My love for you is bitter and disturbing, full of malice and venom. And yet, I do love you.'

She raised her arm and tried to read the time on her wristwatch in the pale ray of light that fell from a street lamp. 'It's nearly eight o'clock. Let's go home.'

'No, no, Hélène!'

He clung on to her clothes, passionately kissed her neck and the delicate soft skin on her arms. 'Hélène, Hélène, I love you, I've never loved anyone but you. Take pity on me, my God, don't send me away. It just isn't possible that you hate me so much! *I* never did anything to hurt you! I'll go away for ever. You wouldn't care?'

'No,' she said cruelly, 'I'm happy. At least, with you gone, my house would be decent and honest again. *She's* old. She'll be forced now to be content with her husband and child. Perhaps one day I'll have a mother like everyone else. You were the cause of my unhappiness.'

He didn't reply. In the darkness of the car she saw him turn his face away and place his trembling hands over his eyes. She leaned forward and told the driver to go back to Paris.

They separated without saying a word. The next day he left for London.

# 8

The following years flowed quickly by. Life was swift, uneasy, tumultuous, like a river that overflows its banks. Later on, when Hélène thought about the two years after Max left, she always pictured them as a torrent of deep, raging water. She had matured, aged during those two years, but her gestures remained brusque and awkward, her face pale, her arms slim and delicate. Among the dazzling young women who wore make-up and jewellery, she seemed to fade into the background, for she was silent, only rarely emerging from her shyness, when she would display a detached, passionate and ironic cheerfulness. But the boys forgave her for being so quiet, for not wearing lipstick, for the indifferent way she accepted their kisses, because she was a good dancer and that was a valued quality at the time, equal to the greatest intelligence and highest moral standards.

After Max's departure and right up until the brief, cold letter in which he announced his marriage, Bella had looked only half awake, subdued and exhausted. Then she had taken lovers she paid for, just like all the other old women. Life was easy, they had millions. It was the happy days when the Stock Market continued to climb towards previously unimaginable heights, when all the tycoons in the world came to Paris, where you could hear people speaking every language on earth. Women of fifty wore dresses known as 'rich kids' that were tight on the hips and revealed their strong legs up to the thigh. It was the age of the first short haircuts, close-cropped, showing off powerful necks adorned by scarves and many strands of pearls. In Deauville, behind closed doors, Englishwomen slipped great wads of pound notes, as thick and crisp as dead leaves, into the hands of handsome young men as swarthy as cigars, tobacco and gingerbread.

Gambling was no longer enough to calm the nerves of Boris Karol; he now needed champagne, women, late suppers, driving fast cars with the top down, throwing money around, the obsequious company of all the parasites in the world, everything he hadn't experienced until that time, everything he had lacked in his youth, which he now latched on to hurriedly, fearfully, as if he could sense that life was flowing through his greedy hands and his time on earth growing shorter with every passing day.

At certain times in the early morning, when make-up was fading from old faces and the last streamers were being crushed underfoot, Hélène would study her father, her mother and the mad crowd around them, and would miss the days gone by when, in spite of everything, she'd had a semblance of a home and a family. She watched her father with clear-sighted despair. The false shirtfront of his dinner suit accentuated the yellowish pallor of his crumpled face. He dyed his moustache now, but the champagne diluted the colour, and his old, sad mouth sagged slightly, its corners pulled tightly into a tense, weary pout. It seemed as if the fire that burned in him had consumed him from within, leaving him nothing more than a brittle skeleton that would crumble in the slightest breeze. Money flowed through his fingers. He personified the terrible image of a man who had realised his dreams. He loved this life so much. He loved the butler's hunched shoulders, the way the little hussy looked at him as she walked past his table, brushing against him and smiling at Bella and Hélène, as if she were thinking, 'You know all about it, don't you? It's the oldest profession in the world, isn't it?'

He smiled at the prostitute, the black jazz players, the professional dancers, his wife's lover . . .

Bella's latest lover was a heavy, gloomy Armenian with oriental, almond-shaped eyes and the fleshy hips of a Mediterranean rug salesman. He amused Karol with his obsequiousness, his loquaciousness, and Hélène recognised the old familiar words that had rocked her to sleep as a child and seemed to be ever present in her life, like a fleeting, enigmatic melody: oil mines, gold mines in Mexico, Brazil, Peru, platinum mines and emerald mines, pearl fisheries, telephones and electric razors, corporations running cinemas, cheese dairies, dye factories, paper mills, tin mines, millions, millions, millions . . .

'I'm the one who did this,' thought Hélène with deadly, sad weariness, 'me. We had Max . . . We would have had Max for ever . . . I wanted to change the course of our lives, as a child might try to stop a flood with his powerless hands, and this is the result: this fat Mediterranean lover, this pale, exhausted man and this old hag.' She looked at her mother with a feeling now devoid of hatred but with a kind of horror, seeing her ravaged, defeated face plastered with make-up, the scarlet line of her thin lips, her face where so many wrinkles, so many tears left their mark and all because of her; she thought all this with pity, terror and remorse. But then she thought hopelessly, 'Everybody lives like this . . .'

She looked around her; so many women pretended to have young bodies but their faces were tragic, lined, scarred, furrowed beneath their make-up. So many men smiled at their wife's lover, so many young girls spun around, like her, carefree and, to all appearances, happy. She thought of her dresses, her suitors, the dancing . . .

She gently touched her father's arm. 'Papa, that's enough champagne. Darling Papa, you'll make yourself ill.'

'Not at all, how silly,' he said impatiently.

One day he said, 'You know, champagne gives you the strength to stay awake.'

'But why stay awake?'

'What else is there to do?' he said with that sad little smile that barely floated across his lips before disappearing.

Hélène looked at the Armenian who was slyly, surreptitiously keeping Karol's champagne glass full. 'Why is he doing that? You'd think he didn't understand that he's old and ill and that wine is bad for him.'

The Armenian had the hips of a female dancer and at the same time possessed the same predatory, cunning graciousness found in characters portrayed in Persian miniatures. He had bluish-black slicked-back hair, a hooked nose and thick raspberry-coloured lips.

'It isn't possible,' thought Hélène, appalled. 'It just isn't possible! He must have sold peanuts in the street when he was young. But he won't hurt Papa. She surely must be paying him. He knows very well that the money comes from Papa. It's in his own best interest to keep Papa around as long as possible.'

One day he looked at her with his bright, insincere eyes with their long eyelashes and said, 'Oh Mademoiselle Hélène, I do love Karol. Now, you won't believe me, but I love him as if he were my father.'

'Does she love him?' wondered Hélène, as her mother danced in the arms of her lover and they passed each other on the brilliant parquet dance floor. 'She's old, she so hates being old; she's buying herself an illusion . . .'

She didn't understand that Bella was looking for something else: that feeling of danger that alone satisfied her and which Max, through his violence and jealousy, was able to quench within her, but the older she got the more she needed to feel stronger, more powerful emotions. She needed to think, 'This man could murder me,' and she would look at the fruit knife in her lover's hand with a sensual shudder of terror.

Her lover, however, wasn't an evil man, but he'd known for some time that Karol, aware of his own obsession with gambling, had put everything he owned in his wife's name to avoid going bankrupt and losing all his money. He didn't have anything against Karol; he was simply carried away by his lavish, florid oriental imagination. He liked Bella, but as a package; in his feelings for her he confused her face with the make-up that covered it, her pearls and diamonds with the furrowed wrinkles of her ageing flesh. He wouldn't have killed Karol but, as he was already ill, he didn't stop himself from giving fate a little push. He dreamed of seeing Karol dead and marrying the widow; he wouldn't waste the money on gambling; in his imagination he constructed images of vast, powerful ventures, allowed himself to get carried away by words like Trust . . . Holding . . . International Finance Company . . . as if they were expressions of love. Oh, he would know how to put Karol's fortune to good use. He'd seduce politicians with wine, beautiful women, excellent meals, by spending money hand over fist . . . He turned his swizzle stick over and over in his fingers, dreaming of mines and oil wells, smiling at Hélène with a look of paternal tenderness that made her shudder.

Karol coughed, in pain, as he so often did recently. The Armenian sadly shook his head: the poor man was clearly completely exhausted. For a moment he tried to imagine a situation in which Karol might play some part, but if that happened everything would be uncertain; the money belonged to Karol, he had given it away and could take it back. He leaned towards Karol, smiled at him affectionately and placed his hand on his arm. 'How about another glass of champagne? It's lovely and cold, delicious . . .'

They went home in the early hours of the morning, Hélène's arms full of dolls and other party novelties.

Bella was tired and yawned. 'They're always the same, these little parties,' she said moodily, 'deadly dull.'

'Then why do you go?' murmured Hélène.

'What else do you want me to do with my time?' Bella said sharply, 'sit around and wait to die . . . or until you get married? You know,' she added with a sudden flash of sincerity, 'women should wait until they are the age I am now to have children . . . Do you think there's anyone in the world who can do without love?'

# 9

In Biarritz, in the morning, when everyone in the luxury hotel was still asleep, Hélène would go out and run along the deserted beach. The hotel's long empty corridors smelled of chilled cigar smoke; the sea breeze blew in through a large bay window open at one side with a clear, sonorous whisper, bringing with it little drops of moisture and the smell of salty air. Every now and then the lift brought up the last of the women, reeling with tiredness, their deep orange rouge fading on their cheeks, and the men in tuxedos whose faces looked green in the morning light.

It was autumn; the beach was empty; the waves rose so high that the sky peeking through them looked moist, iridescent, glistening with a thousand fires.

Hélène went into the sea, and she felt as if the salty water flowing over her body purified her and washed away her tiredness after all the late nights. She lay down in the water, looked at the sky above and laughed, thinking with gratitude, 'It's impossible to be unhappy when you have all this:

the smell of the sea, sand running through your fingers . . . the air, the breeze . . . '

She returned late, happy to feel her cool body beneath her dress, still wet from her swim; she had hastily wrung out her damp hair; nevertheless, she was a little ashamed of herself; she was close to feeling herself foolish in being able to find such perfect pleasure in this innocent way.

Life continued, mad and fast-paced, like an endless, meaningless race towards some invisible finishing point.

A new Russian nightclub had recently opened between Biarritz and Bidart; it was a small house whose walls were covered with crimson satin and the Imperial eagle embroidered in gold. Karol owned shares in the business: the pleasure of drinking was therefore enhanced by paying ten per cent less for every bottle.

That night the Karols were having guests; all around them people were feasting, drinking, loving, thanks to the generosity of Boris Karlovitch Karol. Every now and again a sudden, deep cough severely shook his fragile, beloved old chest, his poor human body, which already seemed to be collapsing, yearning for sleep and peace.

Opposite Hélène, the Grand Duke held court; his presence attracted the Americans like flies to honey. All of his entourage was there, low-ranking princes and authentic ones, both types penniless and greedy, oil merchants, international financiers, weapons manufacturers, professional dancers, former members of the Tsar's Page Corps, women, both expensive and cheap, opium sellers and young girls . . . There wasn't a single face at the table whose anxious, tense features Hélène could not see through its mask of luxury and nonchalance. The lights were low and the beautiful night wafted in through the open bay window.

People also danced outside. The women's dresses and their bodices decorated with jewels shimmered dimly in the dark, like fish scales; the slow dances made them seem as if they were floating at the bottom of an aquarium.

His Highness stood up; the black jazz players, drunk and sentimental, played 'God Save the Tsar' on their horns and cymbals. The august visitor went past a row of servants standing at attention; the women walked behind him, wrapped in their ermine coats and teetering on their high heels from fatigue, boredom and too much wine; the American women stood up; they were drunk; they formed a line and, as the cortège passed, made a deep curtsey as the heir to the Romanovs slowly exited, preceded by a lackey in a powdered wig carrying a flaming silver torch. He stopped in front of the Karols' table, kissed Bella's hand, gave a friendly wave to Karol and left.

'How long have you known him?' asked Hélène.

'Ever since I lent him ten thousand francs,' said Karol, laughing. He had retained his childlike laugh and the joyous grin that spread across his dry, delicate face, but the laughter ended in an aching shudder; he coughed, with less pain than usual, but a look of anguish appeared in his eyes; he took out his handkerchief and wiped his quivering lips; it was damp with blood. He looked at Hélène in terror.

'What's this? I . . . I must have burst a little blood vessel . . . you know? A very tiny blood vessel,' he whispered.

He fell heavily back in his chair, looked around him as if it were the last time he might see these lights, these women, this silvery blue night, but he was strong enough not to say anything, to pay for the last time and smile.

'It's nothing . . . It's just annoying . . . it's just a little blood vessel,' he mumbled to his guests. 'I must have burst a tiny little blood vessel . . . See, it's stopped now . . . See you tomorrow . . .'

# 10

For a little while Boris Karol dragged himself to various spa towns, then to Switzerland. He returned to Paris a dying man. Right up until the last minute he tried to put a brave face on it and not admit defeat. Only once, when he was in a little spa in the Auvergne where the rain streamed down and a gloomy, greenish light peeked through the damp leaves, he said to Hélène, 'It's all over now . . .'

He was standing in front of the wardrobe mirror; he held two ebony brushes that he passed one after the other over his fine white hair, slowly smoothing it down. Suddenly he stopped and walked closer to the mirror; he could see the bright green grass from the lawn outside reflected in it, which made his pale, yellowish face look even more ill, worn out to within inches of death. Hélène sat beside him and listened sadly to the falling rain; he raised one long finger in the air, gave a melancholy smile and whistled an aria from *La Traviata*, softly singing the word, 'Addio . . .'

Then he turned towards Hélène, looked at her almost harshly, nodded and said, 'Yes, my girl, this is the way it is, and neither you nor I can do anything about it.' And he walked out of the room.

Meanwhile they seemed to be losing money everywhere: it went as easily as it had come and for no apparent reason. Karol was still gambling. Spitting up blood, avoiding both the doctors and Hélène, he locked himself away in the shabby little casinos in the spa towns; he gambled and lost every time. Despite feeling that he was going through a bad patch he persisted. He lost money on the Stock Market; he had shares in every business that went bankrupt.

'Fortunately, I've put all the money in Bella's name,' he consoled himself. 'When nothing's left there will still be several million, but we have to hold on to that for the end . . .'

One day in Paris he spat up more blood than usual. Hélène was alone with him. He had just received a letter informing him that a company in which he held the majority of shares had gone bankrupt. He had read it impassively and all he said to Hélène was, 'What rotten luck, eh? But things will work out . . .'

A little while later blood began to spill in waves from his panting mouth. Hélène managed to stop it as the doctor had showed her, then, while he was resting, pale and weak, she ran out to find her mother. She was in the bathroom with the beautician; the smell of cream, herbs and camphor filled the room. Bella was sitting in front of the three-panelled swing mirror and a woman stood in front of her, covering her face with a thick liquid.

Hélène, out of breath, cried, 'Come, come quickly, quickly, he's coughing up blood again . . .'

Bella leaned forward. 'My God, this is so awful!' she said,

sounding very upset. 'Go back to him, quickly! I'm not supposed to move . . .'

'But I'm telling you that he's coughing up blood, you have to come right now!'

'And I'm telling you that I'm not supposed to move. This is a very delicate procedure, she's removing the outer layer of skin from my face and it could get damaged. What are you still doing here?' she shouted angrily. 'Phone the doctor. Make yourself useful instead of standing there like a statue. I'll be there in five minutes.'

When she finally arrived the bleeding had stopped; Karol was calm; he gestured to Hélène. 'Go out, my darling, I need to talk to your mother . . .'

They remained in the room for the rest of the afternoon. A heavy silence filled the apartment. Hélène paced from one window to the other, feeling weak, miserable and lost before the tragic horror of life.

Finally, her mother came out, in tears. 'He wants me to give him back the money he gave me,' she said to Hélène, upset. 'But I don't have any left. Barely a hundred thousand francs. He doesn't know it, but I put everything into that sugar deal where he's just lost all his money. It's his fault! He told me it was a wonderful investment. What can you do? That's the way it goes. But in any case, the poor man wouldn't have been around very long to enjoy the profits.'

'She's such a liar,' thought Hélène. 'She's holding on to the money for her lover.'

'Besides,' Bella continued, 'I don't understand what your father is saying. It isn't possible that he has nothing left, it just isn't . . .'

'Why is it impossible?' Hélène asked coldly.

'Because he had a considerable fortune.'

'Well, he lost it very quickly, that's all there is to it.'

'What can you do?' Bella said again, shrugging her shoulders, 'It's horrible . . .'

She started crying again. In the past she had taken everything she wanted in a grasping, imperious, forceful way, but in the end growing older had broken her down. Men no longer loved her, didn't obey her as they had before. She reverted to habits that returned from long past, during her childhood, when she was a fat little girl spoiled by her doting mother: whining, whims, tantrums, floods of tears that came so easily, groaning and shouting: 'I'm so unhappy! What have I done to God to be punished this way?'

Boris Karol heard what she'd said; he came into the room, barely able to walk; he gently stroked her hair. 'Don't cry, my darling. It will all work out. I'll get better, everything will be fine, we're just going through a bad patch, just a bad patch,' he said again, his voice weak and panting.

When she went out he turned towards Hélène. 'Poor woman, I shouldn't have entrusted her with that money.'

'She's lying, Papa,' said Hélène through clenched teeth.

But he turned and looked at her in a rage. 'Be quiet! How dare you talk about your mother like that?'

Hélène looked at him, sadly, and didn't reply.

'Even if it's true,' he said more softly, 'she's right. I'd lose it all. My luck's deserted me.' He hesitated, then repeated, 'Even if it's true . . .'

He fell silent, but Hélène knew he was thinking, 'Even if it's true, I'd rather not know.'

For a man needs a certain amount of breathable air, a small dose of oxygen and illusion in order to live. He still saw his wife as the proud young woman in a ball dress, the woman who wore lace dressing gowns, put perfume in her long hair and was, to him, the very image of refinement and a happy, luxurious life. He had known other women who were younger or more beautiful, but he had never stopped loving and admiring his own wife. Or perhaps he was simply too proud to admit he'd been defeated, even in his home life. He had always refused to see the truth. Hélène remembered what had happened in St Petersburg when she was still a child and had secretly written words in her schoolbooks that were too obvious, too truthful. He slowly rubbed his eyes.

'Come with me. I want to put my papers in order.'

She followed him into his office.

He gestured to her. 'Take this key,' he said, his voice weak and breathless. 'Open the safe.'

It contained a box of cigars, a bottle of vintage cognac and a few wads of hundred-franc notes in an old purse, a souvenir from his first trip to Monte Carlo. He picked them up, touched them fondly, then pressed them into her hands. 'My darling, take out the piece of paper that's in the yellow envelope and read it out clearly, but keep your voice down . . .'

Hélène read: 'Seventeen thousand shares in the Brazilian Match Corporation . . .'

He hid his face in his hands and replied in a low, monotonous and muffled tone of voice, 'Bankrupt.'

'Belgian Steelworks: twenty-two thousand shares . . .'

'In compulsory liquidation.'

'The thermal baths in Sancta Barbara: twelve thousand shares . . .'

'Bankrupt.'

'The Casino in Bellevue: five thousand shares . . .'

He didn't even bother to reply, just shrugged his shoulders with a weary little smile. She continued to read; at every name, he replied in the same gloomy voice, 'There's nothing we can do at the moment . . .'

Hélène slowly folded up the list. 'That's everything, Papa.'

'Good,' he said, 'thank you, sweetheart. Go to bed now, it's late. There's nothing to be done. It's not my fault, I never dreamed it could be over so fast. Life goes by so quickly . . .'

Hélène left him; he had been sleeping alone since he became ill, in another wing of the house, and he never crossed the sitting room at night, as the doctor had given orders to leave the windows open night and day in order to purify the air. Hélène went back to her room. The lights were on in her mother's bedroom and by going into the bathroom that separated the two back rooms she could see through the glass door, for she had heard the distinct sound of scissors cutting through bundles of thick paper. Bella was sitting on the bed, half naked, her face ready for bed, covered in a mask of cream and her chin held tightly in place by a rubber band. On her knees she had a stack of papers, each folded many times, on which Hélène could read 'National Savings Bank . . .' She was taking some of the dividend coupons from the pile and putting them in an envelope.

'A little present for her lover,' thought Hélène.

She pressed her face to the glass and held her breath, staring at her mother. She felt as if she had never seen her so clearly, looked at her so coldly and calmly. She still had a good figure, attractive arms and shoulders, 'a regal bearing', a body maintained by lotions, massages, exercise, but, just as if someone had glued the head of a different woman on to a decapitated body, above her beautiful, white, plump shoulders rose the neck of a hag. It was on her neck that the forced slimming regimes took their toll; it consisted of a series of rolls of flesh, furrows, in which her strands of pearls sank. Her face bore the marks of all the beauty treatments that should have made it smoother and younger, but which had only succeeded in transforming it into a laboratory, a place to perform experiments. But most of all, what no amount of make-up could hide was the soul of this woman who Hélène knew could be egotistical, harsh and flawed, yet still human, capable of tenderness, even if only towards Max, and which old age had turned to stone, transformed into a monster. Harshness and impatience were visible in her cold eyes, wide open between the little straight lines of her painted eyelashes; evil was obvious in her withered mouth; lies, duplicity, cruelty and cunning showed on her pale, tense, immobile face, even through its mask of make-up.

Very quietly, Hélène walked out. 'Papa has to see this,' she thought, 'he has to get his money back.'

But when she went through the sitting room and saw her father asleep, looked at his pale face and closed eyes, the little exhausted wrinkles round his lips, she realised that he was about to be free and it would happen very soon. She leaned towards him and gently kissed his forehead.

'Is that you, Bella?' he whispered and, without opening his eyes, let out a little sigh of satisfaction and went back to sleep.

He died shortly afterwards. In the hours before, he was calm and slept continuously. He was stretched out in bed; his head had fallen into the space between the bed and the wall; he didn't have the strength to lift it up; it seemed to be pulled down towards the ground by some invisible force. His long, silvery hair fell over his neck. It was a June day, but cold and damp; he impatiently pushed off the covers, revealing his naked feet, deathly pale and icy cold. Hélène took a delicate foot in her hands and tried to warm it up, but in vain.

He waved his hand and pointed to his wallet on the table; he gestured to Hélène to open it. It contained five one-thousand-franc notes. 'For you,' he whispered, 'just for you. It's all I have . . .'

Then he groaned and looked at the window. The nurse closed the curtains.

'Are you going to sleep now, Papa?' asked Hélène.

He sighed. 'To sleep . . .' he said softly.

He put his head in his hand and, at the moment of death, his face took on the sweet, confident smile he'd had as a child. Then he closed his weary eyes, let his body go stiff and went to sleep for ever.

# 11

Karol was buried one cold, rainy summer morning. It was early and very few people managed to get up in time to attend, but the flowers were beautiful.

Hélène felt that not a single tear would find its way from her heart: grief had turned it to stone.

Bella thought she shouldn't wear any make-up, so her face was deathly pale and swollen beneath her crêpe veil. She cried as she raised her damp cheeks to be kissed by the old hags plastered in make-up who looked just like her.

'I'm all alone now,' she said over and over again. 'Ah, no matter what you say, you can't replace a husband. But I can't really cry over him. He suffered so much. He wanted to be at peace . . .'

In the car that took them back to the house she sobbed continuously, but as soon as they were inside she called her lover to come over and they began trying to open the dead man's safe with all his keys.

'Keep going, keep going,' thought Hélène with cold, vengeful joy, recalling the open wardrobe and the empty box she'd seen a few weeks before. 'I'd love to see the look on their faces . . .'

She looked around her and slowly brought her hands to her face. 'What am I doing here?'

She let out a deep groan, but she still couldn't cry. She held both hands to her chest, as if she were trying to push away some weight that was crushing her. In vain. Her heart was as hard and heavy as stone.

'Why should I stay here?' she murmured. 'What am I doing here? What's keeping me here now that the poor man is dead? I'm twenty-one. My father was much younger than I am when he left home. *He* knew how to make a good living. He was just fifteen. He told me about it often. I'm only a girl, but I'm strong and brave.' She clenched her fists.

Above her head she could hear the sound of doors opening and closing. They were obviously going through the rooms that the dead man had occupied, searching the drawers and the pockets of his clothes.

Hélène took the money her father had given her and put it in her bag. She had thrown her hat and crêpe veil on to the bed; she put them on again; her hands were trembling, but one thing and one thing alone concerned her at that very moment: how she would take her cat, Tintabel, away with her. Fortunately, he was still young and very light. She put him in a basket and got out a small suitcase that she filled with clothing. Before leaving, she walked over to the mirror and smiled sadly at her reflection. Pale and thin in her black clothing, the crêpe veil wound round her neck, holding a suitcase in one hand and the cat in the other, she looked like a child of immigrants who'd been forgotten at some port. But at the same time a sense of freedom swelled through her, opening her heart. She breathed more easily, nodding her head.

'Yes, it's the only thing to do. She won't come looking for me. First of all I'm over twenty-one. And besides, she'll be only too happy to be rid of me.'

She rang for the chambermaid. 'Juliette,' she said, 'listen to me carefully. I'm going away. I'm leaving this house for good. You must wait until this evening and then tell my mother that I've gone and that it's pointless looking for me because I'll never come back.'

'Poor Mademoiselle.' The chambermaid sighed.

Hélène felt her heart warm a little; she gave her a kiss.

'I could call a taxi and help you with the suitcase and the cat,' the young maid said. 'Or if Mademoiselle wants to leave him here until tomorrow, you could give me your address and I'll bring him to you?'

'No, no,' Hélène said quickly, holding Tintabel close to her heart.

'Shall I call a taxi?'

But Hélène had no idea whatsoever where she would go and refused once more. She opened the door. 'Go back upstairs, don't make any noise and make sure you say nothing to her before this evening.'

She slipped outside, quickly turned the corner and found herself on the Champs Elysées. She sighed and dropped down on to a bench. The first step was easy. A car. A hotel. A bed.

'I want to sleep,' she thought, but she didn't move. She breathed in the cool, brisk air with sheer delight. She had wrapped her crêpe veil round her neck but the humidity had made it damp and heavy. She had lived confined in the sick man's room for such a long time that she felt an over-whelming desire to breathe in fresh air. She took off one glove, slipped her hand under the cover of the basket and gently stroked the purring cat.

'Fortunately, he isn't heavy. I think I would have stayed rather than leave him behind,' she thought. 'Tintabel, my darling, I'm sure you can't appreciate exactly what saying that means. You'll see, we're going to be happy, you'll see,' she said to the cat.

For the first time, floods of heavy tears flowed down her face. She was alone. The rain had left the Champs Elysées deserted. Little by little she began to warm up; her blood started flowing more quickly, more lightly through her veins.

She raised her head. The wind was picking up. Lights from the little toy stores and sweet shops shone in the rain. It had nearly stopped now; it was just a light drizzle that dried in the wind as it fell. Only the sand on the lower paths was drenched in still, rust-coloured water.

'I never would have left my father,' thought Hélène, 'never. But he's dead, he's at peace now, and as for me, I'm free, free ... free from my house, my childhood, my mother, free from everything I hated, everything that weighed heavily on my heart. That's all in the past now; I'm free. I'll work. I'm young and healthy. I'm not afraid of life.' She looked lovingly at the cloudy sky and the sturdy green trees, their leaves heavy with raindrops; a ray of sunlight appeared between two clouds.

A child passed by; he bit into an apple, looked at the marks his teeth had made and laughed.

'I should go,' thought Hélène.

Then immediately: 'But why? Nothing's keeping me here and I have nothing to go to. I'm free. How peaceful . . .'

She closed her eyes and listened happily to the wind. It was blowing in from the west so must have come from the coast, carrying with it the smell and taste of the sea. Every now and then the clouds would part to reveal an astonishingly warm, bright ray of sunlight, then close up again to form a thick, heavy blanket. But when the sun shone for a moment everything sparkled, the leaves, the tree trunks, the damp benches and the little light drops of glittering water that fell to the earth from the branches. With warmer cheeks, and holding her hands tightly between her knees, Hélène listened to the wind; she strained to hear it as if listening out for a friend's voice. It began softly beneath the Arc de Triomphe, rushed through the tops of the trees making them bend, then surrounded Hélène, whistling and swirling with joy. This strong, cleansing wind cleared away the insipid smell of Paris. It shook the trees so hard it seemed as if some heavy, powerful hand were rocking their trunks, a hand as terrible as the hand of God. The chestnut trees swung back and forth, swishing wildly. The wind dried Hélène's tears, burned her eyes; it seemed to penetrate her head, calmer and lighter now, to warm her very blood. Suddenly she took off her hat, rolled it up in her hand, threw her head back and realised with inexpressible astonishment that she was smiling, that she was gently parting her lips to hold on to the taste of the whistling wind as it swept over her.

'I'm not afraid of life,' she thought. 'The past has given me my first experiences of the world. They have been exceptionally difficult, but they have forged my courage and my pride. And that immutable treasure is mine, belongs to me. I may be alone, but my solitude is powerful and intoxicating.'

She listened to the sound of the wind and felt she could

sense, within its raging, a hidden rhythm, solemn and joyous, like the rhythm of the sea. Its sounds, shrill, raucous and piercing at first, merged into a powerful harmony. She could perceive a sense of growing coherence, like the beginning of a symphony, when the astonished listener hears the first notes of a leitmotif, then loses them and, disappointed, seeks them out once more; then suddenly the theme returns and this time you understand that it will never be lost again, that it is of a different order, more beautiful, more intense, and you listen, reassured and confident as the life-giving tempest crashes against your ears in waves.

She stood up and at that very moment the clouds parted; between the pillars of the Arc de Triomphe, blue sky appeared to light her way.